FIRST ELITE

ONE

Mike Curtis

Dedication

<hr>

This book is dedicated to my amazing sister, Carrie, who saved my life when I believed I had dementia or Alzheimer's. She took me to the hospital, where the doctors discovered I had a brain tumor the size of two tennis balls. She stayed with me when they operated on me for nine hours and cared for me for the next twenty-four days while I recovered.

This book is also dedicated to every man and woman who has served our wonderful nation.

About the Author

Michael Curtis is a U.S. Airforce Vietnam Veteran, Eagle Scout, Grandmaster of Martial Arts, Airline Transport Pilot, and Certified Flight Instructor with over 25,000 hours of flying experience. He has experienced the highest levels of success, from martial arts to flying. Curtis has traveled the world and served as a bodyguard for several well-known individuals. He has lived and worked in Germany, Dubai, India, and the United States. He has held positions at numerous companies, including Eastern Airlines. Curtis has had an amazing life, having flown over all seven continents and around the globe.

First Elite One is a fictional story that eventually became Homeland Security.

Preface

From the unassuming fields of Lewisburg, Tennessee, to the captivating heights of the Vietnamese sky, this is the story of a man who rose from humble beginnings to navigate the corridors of power and influence. His journey is one of resilience, determination, and an unwavering spirit to overcome adversity. From flying dignitaries and celebrities across continents to smuggling drugs and protecting some of the world's most influential figures, this man has witnessed the world's underbelly and walked the path of those who operate in the shadows.

First Elite One is based loosely on real-life events, unveils the covert operations that shape national security, where back channels and blurred lines of morality are the norm. Witness the adrenaline-fueled escapades of a man who has defied expectations and carved a unique path, from martial arts expertise to piloting prowess and a role in the formation of the United States Secret Service.

This is a tale of a small-town boy who dared to dream beyond his circumstances, stepping into a world of intrigue and danger. *First Elite One* is a story of fight, flight, resilience, love, passion, and grief, a tale where the boundaries between right and wrong are often blurred, and the price of loyalty is always too high.

Contents

The Early Years

It was still dark when Jeff climbed out of bed and quickly got done with his daily routines and obligations. He wanted to make it to the barn as quickly as possible and be done with milking the cows and collecting the eggs for breakfast. Uncle Roger was coming over, and Jeff was looking forward to spending time with him.

He quickly dashed out of the room and made his way toward the kitchen; he tiptoed toward it as he didn't want to rouse anyone at this hour. It had been his daily routine since he had turned six to wake up at the break of dawn, get dressed, and then go to the barn. He had even learned to drive a tractor for the men hauling hay at the age of six, and he was now eight years old.

He looked around the kitchen and found some stale bread and only a sliver of homemade butter left in the small dish. Jeff knew better than to take it without asking, or else he would be getting another thrashing from his father. He ate the stale bread and washed it down with water. He was still hungry, but he was looking forward to seeing his Uncle as he knew mommy would definitely be making eggs for breakfast if Uncle was coming over.

Jeff headed outside, once again, tiptoeing around in the dark, his vision clear, as he was used to this routine. But just as he was crossing the living room, he bumped into something hard and fell down with a thud. At that moment, someone got ahold of him by the scruff of his neck.

The smell of alcohol and stale breath made Jeff panic as he knew that he had just bumped into his father, and it was him holding Jeff.

"Where the hell are you off to at this ungodly hour?" his father asked while squeezing his neck painfully.

"T . . . t . . . to the b . . . b . . . barn . . .. It's time to milk the cows," Jeff stuttered.

"Don't you dare lie to me, you brat . . ." his father shouted, as he let go of Jeff but kicked him as he did so. Jeff stumbled away, tears streaming down his face.

"I . . . I'm not l . . . lyin' . . . I do this every day. You can ask mommy or even Fred. I help him milk the cows, collect eggs, and sort out piles of hay . . . " he tried explaining.

"You dare answer me . . . let me tell ya, who's boss around here . . . " his father's words slurred as he took out his belt to beat Jeff up.

Jeff knew it was pointless to say anything; his father was beyond reason. After having drunk a fifth of Old Charter, the man was simply too far gone to listen to his son's pleas. Besides, by now, Jeff had gotten used to his father's beatings. Most times, he was used as a punching bag for his father to vent out his frustration of not having enough money, for failing to be a good father and simply being a miserable man.

His father thrashed Jeff a couple of times, cursing him until he was completely exhausted and fell back on the worn-out sofa that he had been slumbering on earlier before passing out, completely indifferent to his eight-year-old son's sobs. Jeff looked at his father miserably, then, wincing, limped out of the house, his whole body aching from the belting he had received.

By now, the sky was a beautiful shade of indigo and blood orange, casting an amber glow on the entire barnyard. Some of the cows were grazing near the shed, which was a dilapidated building sorely in need of a fresh coat of paint. Next to it was the portable house for brooder chickens that Uncle Roger and Grandfather had invested in.

"Aye, boy . . . you're late today," Uncle Roger hollered as he came out of the portable house bearing fresh eggs.

"Yeah, I ran into Pa . . . " he shrugged and slowly made his way toward the barn shed, trying not to limp, too exhausted to show enthusiasm for his Uncle. Roger looked at him closely and then swore.

"For Pete's sake, come lemme have a look at ya," he carefully placed the eggs in a nearby basket, then took hold of Jeff's arm.

"It's alright. I am fine . . . gotta milk the cows."

"The cows ain't goin' anywhere . . . now, be still and lemme see," Roger shushed him and inspected the bruising on Jeff's arms and legs, as well as his swollen forehead.

He then gently guided Jeff inside the shed and made him sit on a stack of hay, then ordered Fred, the farm boy, who must be around 15-16 years old, to get him a clean, cold, wet cloth and ointment. Jeff looked passively at the large shed where bales of hay were stacked in one corner. Some of the cows were inside, ready to be milked. His Uncle remained quiet as he closely inspected his nephew's wounds.

Fred came back with a wet towel and ointment and handed it over. Roger gently wiped down Jeff's face, then started putting the ointment on the bruises, whereas Fred went back to stacking the hay.

"Lemme guess, he once again got tanked and crashed on the sofa?" he asked.

Jeff nodded his head in anguish, trying to hold back tears, as he wanted to be brave in front of his Uncle.

"The old fool will seriously drown in that bottle one day."

"How's aunty?" Jeff changed the subject, making Roger stop mid-tirade.

"She's fine and sent your favorite bottle of apple jam. We'll take it up to the house once we're done with all the chores."

"She sent the jam?" Jeff perked up.

"Yeah!"

"But why are you here so early? Gramps is still asleep, and mommy said you'll be comin' by around breakfast time."

"Yeah . . . but I wanted to help around with some of the chores before breakfast. Besides, I am gonna be headin' to Nashville later in the day and won't be back till tomorrow."

"Really, can I come with ya? I've never been outside Lewisburg ever," Jeff asked excitedly.

"Nah . . . not this time. But I'll take ya with me some day. I promise, now c'mon, help milk the cows; then I gotta surprise for ya." Roger patted him on the head, ruffling his hair.

The smell of frying eggs, baked bread, and coffee hit Jeff as he entered the house, his mouth watering and stomach rumbling with hunger. He was glad his Uncle was visiting, and, thanks to him, they would all get to have a good meal today.

"C'mon along, get seated; the food's pipin' hot," his mother beckoned them toward the table, where his Grandfather was already seated.

"How are ya, pops?" Roger asked as he took a seat across from him.

"Same old joint pain," he grimaced.

"Thanks for the flour sack and the jam; it was mighty kind of ya to bring it over. It's been a tough few weeks," Jeff's mother put a plate of sunny side-ups in front of his Uncle and fetched fresh coffee for him, then put a plate of eggs in front of Jeff, too.

"No issues; I understand old Billy Haddock owes ya money for corn?" Roger raised an eyebrow.

"Yeah … I was meanin' to collect it, but … " she simply shrugged, leaving the sentence unfinished.

"Don't worry, I'll get it sorted. Is he up or still sleepin'?" he asked about his brother.

"Sleeping, it's better that way," she grimaced, and they all nodded, knowing this was the only way to maintain peace in the household.

Jeff's father was a violent man who was even meaner when drunk. His father and Grandfather jointly owned the farm, but it was Jeff's Uncle and Grandfather who took care of the farm mostly, especially since the accident in 1962 when Jeff's father lost his eye, spearing tobacco. The spear broke off as he was putting the tobacco on it and landed in his eye. He was rushed to the hospital, where treatment was denied as he had no insurance, and was then sent to Nashville, where he lost his eye even after a $250,000 surgery, money they said could have been saved if he had received immediate care.

The family was poor, and they didn't have that kind of money; they usually grew their own food and sold some of the products like milk, eggs, and corn in the local market to live. Lewisburg was a small city in Tennessee, and in the '50s and '60s, it wasn't truly developed. The incident had made Jeff's father more bitter and resentful, making him resort to being on his own or simply drinking. Jeff was the collateral damage in this turn of events as he was mostly beaten for something or the other, as an excuse by his father to vent his frustration.

After breakfast was over, Uncle Roger and Grandpa started discussing the new harvest and the impending storm that was heading Tennessee's way, whereas Jeff helped his mother clear up the dishes and wash them too.

"I heard your father yelling at you around dawn, but I didn't know he hit you again," his mother whispered.

"It's okay, mommy. I bumped into him, and he woke up," he shrugged.

"Oh, honey ... I'm sorry," she kneeled down and hugged him.

Jeff remained quiet but returned his mother's embrace. He knew she couldn't do anything for him, nor could she save him from his father's fists, but just her love and constant reassurance were enough for Jeff.

"Enough of the coddling, c'mon, Jeff, let's go." His Uncle came in the kitchen and motioned him to get going.

Jeff was excited and felt like a grown-up as his Uncle taught him how to plant corn in the field through a tractor. They both sat on the tractor as his Uncle navigated through the corn field and showed Jeff the right way of planting the corn. It took Jeff a couple of failed attempts before he was finally able to plant an entire row of corn in the field.

This was now another task that he looked forward to, apart from doing other chores around the farm. By now, the sun was glaring at the top of their heads, and the entire field was bathed in a golden glow. After planting corn, both the Uncle and nephew made their way toward the shed, where his Grandfather was going over the ledger with Fred. Seeing them, Fred poured them both a glass of cold water that they both gulped down.

"How's it going ... pops, do the numbers tally?" Roger asked.

"Look for yourself," his Grandfather passed on the ledger to his Uncle, who looked at it with a frown.

"It seems we owe more than we earned. It ain't lookin' good."

"Yeah, I suppose we could always sell some cows . . ."

"Probably, but things need to pick up, and that son of yours needs to start pullin' his weight. Either you talk to him, or I'll have to," he said angrily.

"I'll talk to him. You will only further aggravate him."

"Like I care," he stomped his feet and walked away.

"Wait a while, let him cool off. Now, tell me, what did ya learn today?" Jeff's Grandfather stopped him from going after his Uncle, so Jeff sat back and told his Grandfather everything about that day. His Grandfather listened attentively. For Jeff, both his Grandfather and Uncle were the father figures who taught him everything, instead of his own father.

After a while, Roger joined them and told Jeff and his father about the J-3 Cub aircraft he had recently purchased and was going to Nashville to finalize the deal. The J-3 Cub was an American light aircraft that was built between 1938 and 1947 by Piper Aircraft. The aircraft had a simple, lightweight design, which gave it good low-speed handling properties and short-field performance.

"I got a sweet deal cuz the plane needs to be assembled," Roger explained.

"Oh, Uncle, please lemme help ya, please, I wanna learn everything about a plane," Jeff said excitedly, his interest piqued.

"Course' kiddo ... don't worry, once I've got all the parts, I'll make ya learn all about them planes." His Uncle patted him on the back affectionately, and Jeff did a happy dance, making both the men laugh.

The family rarely got to have such merry times, but both men were glad to see Jeff happy, for the boy was always getting scolded or was mostly hard at work around the farm, even at such a young age. They were glad that they had seen to taking care of his upbringing, for had they left Jeff to his own devices or at the mercy of his father, God only knows what the outcome would have been.

Soaring High

"I need the money, and I want it now. What happened to the recent crop that we sold in the market?" Jeff's father argued.

"We had to pay half of the money to those we were indebted to; some went to settling your tab at the tavern, and the rest was used to buy more seedlings and chicken feed for the farm," Grandfather told him, trying to remain calm.

"What do ya mean, settlin' my tab? Did Barny threaten ya?"

"No, he didn't, and don't ya dare go pickin' fights in town. We are already sufferin' enough.

Your brother Roger went for a brew, and he came to know about the running tab, so he settled it."

"That fool, why can't he keep his nose outta my business?"

"You idiot, if he doesn't keep track of your business, we will all be out on the streets; you should be thanking him for lookin' out for us. He runs his own farm *and* looks after ours."

"I don't need no helpin'; I can do it on my own," Jeff's father thundered.

"Yeah, right! You can't say sober for a full whole day; you'll manage the farm, as if. Had it been up to you, we would starve for days." Grandfather angrily said as he stood up with the support of his cane and walked out. Leaving his son seething in anger.

Jeff knew this was his cue to get out of the house, as he would be his father's punching bag for all the pent-up anger he was bottling. He tiptoed toward the exit and made a run for the door, not bothering to stop or look back as his father hollered his name.

His Uncle was in the shed when Jeff reached his farm. Uncle Roger's farm was just three miles ahead of theirs and was a little bigger and in good condition. Instead of having a dilapidated outhouse and chicken coop like theirs, the buildings were well-kept.

Roger was an astute man and good with numbers; he was also different from Jeff's father and had worked beside his father from a young age. He had requested his father to give him his share of the farm so Roger could strike out on his own, which he had done. Through smart farming and money saving, he had been able to make a success out of his farm and wanted to venture toward cattle rearing. Although, his one indulgence was planes.

Even now, he was working on assembling the J-3 Cub plane that he had bought a few months ago. He was cleaning and oiling one of the wings.

"Hello, Uncle," Jeff greeted him as he excitedly looked at the parts strewn around.

"Hello, Jeff, glad to see ya, boy; I was thinkin' of taking a break," his Uncle told him, rubbing his hand with a stained towel.

"Father was in a foul mood; he had an argument with Grandpa over money, so I decided to scoot. Otherwise, I would get a beating," Jeff explained.

"Oh! Well, ya did a good thing. Why were they arguing about money?" he asked.

"Umm . . . he wanted money, and Grandpa said there ain't none. Plus, he was mad at you settlin' the bill at the tavern."

"I see! Anyway, I hope you're hungry. Your aunt cooked up some hearty stew. Let's have that, and then I'll show ya a thing or two about planes," his Uncle said as they both made their way toward the main house.

As his Uncle had said, the stew was hearty and delicious, and Jeff took second helpings since his Uncle's house was the only place where he could do so and eat to his heart's content. At his home, the food was always little, and most of the food they ate, they grew themselves. The meat was only for his father and Grandfather. The others could only eat a few morsels of it.

After lunch, his Uncle took him back to the shed and started explaining the ins and outs of assembling a plane and servicing it properly, oiling the parts, and checking them for rusting. Then he taught him how to apply a fresh coat of paint and put decals on it.

In the course of a few months, Jeff would often skip to his Uncle's farm to help him with the plane once he was done with all his chores. He had now been helping Fred more since last year as his father had also started a guitar-playing gig in the town to earn extra cash. He was rarely on the farm, so the additional responsibilities fell on the shoulders of the nine-year-old boy.

Jeff liked it, for this kept him out of his father's way, which was equal to keeping away from harm's way.

It was raining heavily, and Jeff had been working tirelessly to herd all the cattle inside the old barn so as to avoid any of them getting sick with cold. The rain had come after a long period of drought. They were worried if it didn't rain, the entire harvest would be ruined, but now that the rain was here, it was torrential and made all the farmers worry that their fields might get flooded.

Once Jeff was finished, he wearily made his way to the main house, going straight to the kitchen to see if there were any leftovers. He found a small plate hidden behind the flour can and quickly said a prayer of thanks. His mother had saved some goulash for him. Jeff hungrily ate it with a stale piece of bread and washed it all down with some lemonade, which was also tucked behind a large jar.

His mother loved him and always tried to look out for him, and these were the small ways she made sure Jeff was fed. She couldn't save him from his father's wrath, which resulted in him turning on her. Jeff sighed as he washed away the dishes and was wiping the counter when someone grabbed him by his hair and spun him around.

"Stealin' food, are we?" his father's words slurred.

"N . . . n . . . no . . . father. I was just cleaning the kitchen," Jeff choked, shivering with fear.

"You lyin' to me, you filthy boy. You're nothin' but a burden. Lemme teach you a lesson," his father grabbed him and pulled him outside.

Jeff tried to wrestle himself away from his father, but his grip was firm, and his father started punching him. Jeff tried to defend himself by escaping. He pushed his father away a little to dash out, but his father stumbled a little, getting angered further. He was raging drunk and furious; he saw the guitar lying nearby and picked it up, swinging it toward his son.

"Please, father, leave me be. I swear, I wasn't stealing. Please…" Jeff pleaded, but his father was beyond reasoning; he kicked Jeff and raised the guitar, bringing it down on his back. Jeff screamed as the guitar hit him on his tailbone. His father once again hit him on the back, this time shattering the guitar with the blow. A feral sound escaped Jeff's mouth, his screams echoing in the dark. A loud thunder cracked outside, and Jeff's mother rushed downstairs. His Grandfather also came out of his room.

His father was fuming and heaving, yelling obscenities at his son until his Grandfather pushed him away, and Jeff cowered in his mother's arms.

"You animal, get away from him, or you'll kill the child," his Grandfather shouted.

Jeff looked at his father with pure hatred. His whole being centered on the fact that he could never let his father or anyone hurt him ever again, the way he had been hurt at that moment. He was determined never to let himself be cornered or feel so weak and small ever again.

That night, while his mother tended to his wounds, tears streamed down Jeff's face due to the immense pain he was in and the humiliation he had felt.

He didn't want to be weak anymore; he wanted to stand up for himself and no longer be vulnerable to violence. He needed to become stronger and learn to protect himself. He decided to learn karate or any other martial arts that would help him.

Uncle Roger came to see Jeff, and seeing his bruised and battered nephew made him teary-eyed. Both his Uncle and aunt requested his mother to let Jeff come away with them for a while until he was healed since he was of no help around the farm in his condition.

His mother relented, and Jeff happily went to his Uncle's farm. There, with healthy meals and constant medical care, Jeff's injuries healed. He had been lucky not to have incurred any lasting damage on his spinal cord, and no bones had been broken. Only his skin had ruptured and welted, which healed with proper ointment.

During his healing process, his Uncle started teaching him about flying planes and would take Jeff out with him for a ride in the J-3 Cub. He was teaching his nephew how to fly a plane. At the same time, Jeff told his Uncle that he wanted to learn Karate and would appreciate it if he would help him out.

His Uncle understood and found a place in town where Jeff could go and learn Karate. The place was a little shabby, but his teacher was a black belt and good at his job. He also knew of Jeff's background and was well aware of his father's anger issues.

"Let me be very clear, boy. A lot of Karate teachers teach a watered-down style, with no hip action and no depth of punching. They keep it easy, but know this: you are what your teacher is, and if he knows a lot, you should be able to demonstrate this knowledge," his teacher, Master Jonatan Yoko, a Japanese American man, told him.

Jeff liked the discipline that Karate provided in his life. For him, the movements, the hip inflection, presence of mind, and efficient motor skills, along with heightened senses, were very peaceful growth experiences for him.

Master Jonatan Yoko himself was impressed by the 10-year-old boy's enthusiasm and ability to learn. In only a few months, Jeff had shown real aptitude for this form of martial arts.

Along with Karate, Jeff also learned to fly an airplane as he had been keenly observing his Uncle during their rides together. Jeff and his Uncle had a flying handbook with all the procedures printed in it, so they learned to fly together. One day, Jeff insisted his Uncle let him fly for a while. Of course, it was going to be co-piloting.

"Let's see what ya got, boy; either you'll soar us high, or we'll be crashing to the ground." His Uncle laughed as he conceded.

Much to his surprise and delight, Jeff turned out to be a good co-pilot. His flying skills were remarkable. After that, Uncle Roger encouraged him to fly more, but never alone.

The boy was a marvel, for at the age of ten, he was flying an airplane, and when Jeff flew the aircraft around the field, the cows always headed to the barn, just knowing it was milking time. This was kind of a ritual that had made them attuned to the pattern.

"I'm so proud of him, Pa, and so glad he's nothin' like his old man. I've always dreaded what would happen if Jeff turned out to be just like my brother. A bitter, violent man with no prospects," Roger said one day.

"He's a bright boy and nothing like his father. We are raising Jeff, not him. I'm sure he will make something of himself. He has a knack for learnin' things. I've heard he's happy to be joinin' Boy Scouts," he inquired.

"Yeah, a couple of boys he's friends with are in it, so I encouraged him to go for it; that would teach him balance, leadership skills, as well as life skills. Plus it will help him build a sense of community." Roger shrugged, and his father nodded.

The whole premise of Boy Scouts is groups of 6-7 boys, ranging from age 11-14, organizing themselves into small natural subgroups under a boy leader. Their training consisted of tracking and reconnaissance, mapping, signaling, knotting, first aid, and all the skills that arise from camping and similar outdoor activities. To become a Scout, a boy would promise to be loyal to his country, help other people, and, in general, obey the Scout law; this in itself was a simple code of chivalrous behavior easily understood by the boy. This gave them a sense of camaraderie and helped them understand the meaning of public service and brotherhood.

For Jeff, this was a golden opportunity, and he truly thrived in it. He was a brilliant Boy Scout and rose up to the rank of an Eagle Scout. Jeff's appetite for learning was something that would take him very far.

Vietnam

"Dude, just roll it and take a drag; this ain't no basic spliff. It's a doobie." Charlie told Jeff, urging him to do it.

"I don't know, man, I still don't like dope that y'all are so hung up on . . . so forgive me if I don't trust your recommendation," Jeff eyed him skeptically.

They had just gotten done with patrol duty and were now drinking cold beer and getting high as they sat behind an old building. The past few days had been a flurry of activity. The scouts went hiking through the woods at Tennessee State Park. Mercifully, it wasn't that cold, and the experience was good, although chaperoning the newbies was a task that Jeff could certainly do without. No matter how good he was at it.

However, they were now being trained to hike through the Walls of Jericho Trail, which was difficult. Jeff looked forward to the challenge of it. He was bored out of his mind from all the mundane activities that they had to do, especially the jousting, pumpkin throwing, and canoeing around the lake type activities that they usually did, especially during national training courses and the overnight or three-day camps that were conducted on district level.

Initially, when Jeff had joined the Boy Scouts, he had been excited and full of energy to learn new things, and mind you, he had learned so much from tying knots to building fires, outdoor camping, trailing and trekking through forests, and even climbing a mountain. All these skills had been instrumental, and since he always had an aptitude for learning, he had risen through the ranks pretty quickly; from the Star merit badge, he had advanced to Life. This was primarily due to the CPR and lifesaving skills that he had acquired not only through learning from Boy Scouts but also from his life at the farm.

While working at the farm, he had assisted many foal births as well as helped in putting down the ailing animals. He often assisted with suturing and other medical procedures. So, it had been a little easier for him to learn treating a victim of shock, burns, cuts, and bleeding. It was also required for those aspiring to reach the Eagle badge, Second Class, or First Class, which was the most coveted and near impossible to earn, to showcase their knowledge of first aid by treating a victim of respiratory and cardiac emergencies or a victim of heat and cold-related emergencies.

Jeff had, so far, learned about treating bites and stings, burn victims, CPR, and basic first aid, as well as shocks, burns, and cuts. He and Charlie were also pros at the patrol method, as well as camping and hiking. Thence, they were leading the groups through trails most of the time.

"Trust me, you're gonna like it and be flyin' soon. Just try. Here, lemme roll it for ya. This is not just cannabis and tobacco; it's pure marijuana," he explained to Jeff as he handed it to him, and Jeff took a drag, raising a brow.

"What is it?" Jeff asked.

"It's a doobie. It's the new thing around the block; told ya you'd like it," Charlie laughed as Jeff took another drag.

Jeff felt more relaxed than he had ever been and more at peace. He also felt a Zen-like feeling enveloping him. He closed his eyes and relished the feeling. Charlie also went silent beside him, both friends taking drags and then sipping their beers.

Jeff had been looking forward to this week as it was his birthday. In the past few months, his time had been divided between the farm and Boy Scout's training camps. That day, he had been working at the farm when his Uncle arrived with some surplus wheat bags for them and asked Jeff to store them.

"Happy Birthday, Jeffy boy. How's the Scout trainin' going?"

"It's goin' well," he replied.

"Good . . . so what's the plan for today?"

"Nothin,' I'll just be hanging out with some friends," he simply shrugged.

"Hmm. And how are things at home? I heard you argued with your old man?"

"Yeah, he thought I was the same 10-year-old, afraid of his fists. Had to teach him the hard way; that's not the case no more," Jeff said bitterly, thinking of the ugly fight between he and his father. His father tried to smash a beer bottle on Jeff's head just because Jeff stopped him from hitting his mom. He had to twist his father's arm and then bring him to his knees, putting pressure on his back until his father collapsed. At that moment, Jeff felt validated. He was no longer a weakling. Over the years, he had grown taller and filled out. He towered over his father, and ever since learning Karate and Taekwondo, he had been defending himself, but this time, he had been on the offense, and it felt great.

"I won't say what you did was right, but perhaps he needed that lesson. Anyway, I heard you are now on the sixth level and about to get the purple belt?" Uncle Roger asked.

"Yeah, I've been practicing hard and aiming to get a brown belt in the next two years," Jeff told him.

"What about the flyin' lessons? Are you taking them? I know you were saving from them, but if ya need me to lend you some dough, lemme know," he offered.

"Nah, I got some savings, so I'll be applying soon," Jeff refused.

"I see; anyway, here's your birthday gift," his Uncle handed him an envelope from the back of his pocket, and Jeff took it.

"Before you refuse, let the first lesson be on me; you can pay for the rest," his Uncle stopped Jeff from arguing and patted him on the shoulder.

Jeff nodded, trying to remain calm and stoic. Displays of emotions were not a thing in their family.

Jeff celebrated his 16th birthday with his Boy Scouts friends. Alec had gotten them fake IDs, and they were hitting a questionable pub with lax policies located on the outskirts of Nashville. They all entered the old pub with swagger, Jeff wearing his favorite bootleg jeans, thrifted cowboy shoes, and the checkered blue shirt. His hair was combed back, and he was even wearing his Grandpa's Old Spice cologne.

The pub was full when they entered, the interior all dark wood. The smells of sweat, alcohol, and cheap perfume permeated the air. Jeff looked around and saw another group of underage guys drinking beer and looking around, awed. There was a pool table in the far corner, and some biker dudes were playing. Along with them were some scantily dressed women just hanging around. Jeff's eyes widened at so much display of skin.

In his sixteen years, all he had experimented with was with drugs and booze, and occasionally fooling around with a girl or two around his neighborhood and school. To see women in tight-fitted dresses, displays of cleavage, and people making out in dark corners was quite a new experience for the sixteen-year-old boys.

Jeff and his buddies ordered their drinks, this time opting for brandy and whiskey instead of the regular beer. As Alec had said, "Tonight is the night to upgrade and elevate our alcohol consumption." The first sip of whiskey made Jeff choke, but he remained true to it and downed the whole glass.

That night, they partied hard, drinking and eating burgers, then later gorging the cake they had bought from a convenience store. By this time, Jeff was completely wasted, so Bryan and Alec offered him to crash at their place.

Once he was at their place, the boys offered him some shrooms.

"Tonight's the night to experiment with it all. You've been doin' joint and doobie for a while now. The next step is to try shrooms, my friend. You're gonna be singing to the high heavens after it," Bryan sniggered, and Alec started laughing.

They convinced him to try the shrooms, and they put the powder into pill capsules. "This is to avoid the taste of mushrooms altogether; it tastes nasty and earthy, my friend; you're not gonna like it," Alec said.

The thing with mushrooms is that it's a psychedelic drug, best known for hallucinations and sound enhancement. It is often taken for enhancing one's creativity, and artists especially prefer it. For Jeff, the shrooms were an altogether different experience. His body felt as light as a feather; he could see the room morphing into rippling waves, and the texture of everything he touched somehow felt like cotton. Alec and Bryan put on a Rolling Stones record, and the sound felt enhanced. All in all, the shrooms were like a psychedelic dream.

This was how Jeff got hooked on drugs and booze in the scouts. He was still diligent when it came to his scouting duties. Sharp as a whistle when learning at flying school and helping on the farm. But once he was out with the boys or done with his chores, he would either dope or do the shrooms. By the time he turned 18, he had even experimented with cocaine and heroin.

"I got my pilot's license," Jeff told his mother, walking into the kitchen one day as she prepared lunch.

"Oh my, I'm so glad, hon." His mother croaked happily as she hugged him, and he returned her embrace.

"Yeah … I'll go tell Grandpa and Uncle Roger; they've been waiting for the news."

"What about your father? Aren't you gonna tell him?" she asked.

"Like he would care," he said, rolling his eyes.

"Don't be like that, I'm sure he'll be happy for ya."

"No, he won't, and you know it. Besides, it ain't any of his business," Jeff rebuked, leaving his mother upset and heading for the shed where his Uncle and Grandfather would be.

The two men were deep in conversation when Jeff sauntered in.

"I've got good news for ya both," he smiled.

"Well, we could definitely do with some good news ... " his Uncle smiled, although it didn't reach his eyes. Something was troubling him. Jeff then looked at his Grandfather, and he looked grave.

"Is somethin' wrong?" Jeff couldn't help but ask.

"Nah, tell us the news," his Uncle insisted.

"Well, I got my license," he said nonchalantly.

"No shit! That's great news … man, I'm so proud of you," his Uncle beamed and thumped him on the back.

"Glad to hear this, Jeffy," his Grandfather smiled, getting teary-eyed. Jeff went and hugged him.

"I've got one more piece of news," he said coyly.

They both looked at him with raised brows, "I made it to the position of an Eagle Scout," Jeff beamed.

"You did … ? I knew you could do it; I saw how hard you worked for your service project and how much of a good troop guide you were," his Uncle appraised him.

To achieve the Eagle Scout Rank, one had to complete an additional ten merit badges, bringing the total number of badges up to 21. Out of these, 13 had to be from specific categories.

The merit badges included the following: First Aid, Citizenship in the Community, Citizenship in the Nation, Citizenship in the World, Communication, Cooking, Personal Fitness, Emergency Preparedness or Lifesaving, Environmental Science or Sustainability, Personal

Management, Swimming, Hiking or Cycling, Camping, and Family Life.

Jeff had been an active life scout for six months. He worked on his service proposal side by side, which was to revamp and refurbish the old gymnasium at the local high school since its dreary condition made it difficult for the local varsity to practice efficiently there. Under his leadership, his scouts managed community donations with their own strategic planning. To get the Eagle Scout title was a great honor, and Jeff was proud of himself.

"You have really made us proud, Jeff; I'm so glad you turned out to be different from your old man," his Grandfather's voice choked, once again, tears flowing down his face. Jeff frowned. He had never seen his Grandpa getting this emotional.

"What's really goin' on, Pa? I've never seen you like this," he asked.

"Ask him, Roger," said his Grandpa.

Jeff looked at his Uncle, who himself seemed sad and angry. He took some papers from his jacket and handed them to Jeff, who looked enquiringly at him.

"Did you register to get drafted into the military?" his Uncle asked.

"Umm . . . yeah."

"I see. I wish you would have discussed it with me."

"I didn't think there was anything to discuss. I'm eighteen, and it's the law. Besides, I wanted to serve my country in Vietnam. There's a war going on, and our troops are stationed there," Jeff explained.

"But why is the war goin' on?" his Grandfather asked.

"To stop the spread of communism, apparently. Don't know what that shit is!" Uncle Roger shrugged.

"When do I leave?" Jeff asked, trying to remain in control.

"End of this week. I wish you woulda told us. We would have had time to process this," his Uncle said.

"That's why I didn't tell y'all. I didn't want to prolong the goodbyes," he said firmly, then took the draft papers from his Uncle's hand and left, leaving the two men looking sadly at Jeff's retreating back.

Jeff's recruitment into the war was an emotional situation for his family. His father didn't care, but his mother kept crying the whole week. She was afraid that she might lose her son to the war and never see him again. His Uncle and aunt visited him daily. Jeff felt a sense of trepidation as well as excitement as some of his Boy Scouts friends had also been recruited to fight in the war.

He was transported to Nashville for the Army. His first few weeks in the barracks were tough, the gruesome hours and amount of exercise and drills utterly consuming. Had he not been a farm boy and a scout, used to the hard work and early hours, Jeff would not have lasted in the Army. The sheer discipline it took to remain there was commendable.

He was being trained like a normal Army soldier, but when they found out he was a pilot with 880 hours, he was moved to the Air Force. He went to Lackland Air Force Base for basic training and OTS (Officer Training School) and then to Minot, North Dakota. All this stationing was instrumental in his piloting skills as well as his rise through the ranks. Jeff also liked going from place to place. From never having stepped a foot out of Nashville to flying across the U.S. skies, then being stationed in Saigon to train for the F-4 Phantom Jet, Jeff had a variety of new experiences.

The F-4 Phantom is a tandem-seat fighter-bomber designed as a carrier-based interceptor to fill the U.S. Navy's fleet defense fighter role. It was a special fighter plane and needed extensive training, which Jeff excelled in. However, coming to Saigon was a difficult transition. Once he became good at flying the F-4 Phantom Jet, carrying out some important missions, and getting further trained, he was sent to Da Nang to join the 366 Tactical Fighter Wing.

Da Nang

It was one of those days when Jeff questioned his sanity for agreeing to join the USAF (United States Air Force), repeatedly putting his life on the line. He looked at the terrain around him and sighed. He was a long way from home and wondered how everyone was doing. He missed his family, even his sorry excuse of a father. He hadn't gone back even once after joining the forces.

From people to language, food, customs, and traditions, Vietnam was a culture shock for Jeff. It was all so far removed from his former life that even now, after having experienced Saigon, getting lost in the dense forests of Vietnam, and then being posted at Da Nang Air Base and fighting under the

366 Tactical Fighter Wing division, Jeff still felt alienated from this reality at times.

To say being in a war zone was dangerous and overwhelming would be an understatement. There was constant bombardment by the enemy, and the threat of walking into a death trap while hiking through Vietnamese mountains or crossing the Han River, stepping into a landmine laid out by the North Vietnamese, or even flying the plane under the radar, was usually a death risk.

Constantly being vigilant and being on guard, as well as living with the fear of death lurking around the corner was mentally taxing. Every time Jeff flew the fighter jet, navigating through the skies was difficult because the attack by the Northern Vietnamese would start incessantly. It had become extremely difficult for him to do so.

The 366th Tactical Fighter wing arrived at Phan Rang Air Base in March 1966. It was an air base used by the Japanese and French during World War II. Due to the prolongment of the Vietnam War, Phan Rang was expanded by the USAF in 1966 to accommodate both American and South Vietnamese fighter and helicopter units. The base was a joint operation by the United States Marine

Corps (USMC), the United States Army, the Army of the Republic of Vietnam (ARVN), and the Republic of Korea Marine Corps (ROKMC).

The North Vietnamese Army had launched a murderous campaign against the South, and both USMC and USAF were countering it.

Jeff's current rank was 1Lt., and he had only recently been promoted. Earlier, while flying a fighter jet, he had to commence dogfighting when an enemy plane came within three miles of his radius. He had to make some stressful maneuvers to get the upper hand in the fight. Thankfully, Jeff was physically fit to perform the aerial combat.

"I'm impressed, man! No wonder you're called an ace. The way you flex your legs and torso to keep blood from draining out of the head during aerial combat is superb. And thanks for helping me with my physical maneuvers, too. But no one does the "grunt" better than you." Timothy handed Jeff a cigarette as they sat against a tree, looking at the dense forest. This was their resting spot; usually, Jeff would come into the woods to find some peace and a semblance of normalcy amidst the madness.

"I saw some of the petrol guys smoking Thuốc lào through a waterpipe or something. They confiscated it from some Vietnamese trespassers earlier this week. I've heard that stuff is potent," Timothy told him. Jeff simply nodded, not saying anything. Timothy Adams was 2Lt. Jeff's junior from Idaho.

"I've heard the northerners gave acquired Soviet MRLs (multiple rocket launchers)," he spoke after a while.

"Yeah . . . talk about actually gettin' toasted. From fearing their bombardment every week to now becoming a target of a rocket launcher. Just what we need!" Jeff grimaced as sirens started blaring, indicating it was time for their infantry's patrol duties at the fixed defensive positions.

"Tell Janine I love her and was gonna marry her. Heck, I wrote her a letter too. . . in my bag . . . give her the letter. And all my other remaining stuff to momma . . . promise me!" Timothy panted, blood oozing from the gash on the side of his neck and from his chest. A piece of shell fragment was protruding from his chest, and a small shrapnel could be seen embedded on the side of his neck.

"Just hang in there, man. I'll take you to the infirmary; don't give up on me . . . " Jeff implored in a panicked voice. They both had been on the way back to the main base when they saw enemy troops entering from the eastern side. Immediately, the two opened fire and asked for backup.

They took down most of the enemy troops when a mortar hit the line of trees behind which they were taking cover. Jeff had seen the mortar hurtling toward them and yelled for Timothy to jump the other way. Unfortunately, Timothy took just a couple of seconds to take cover. The mortar hit where he was, and the injuries Timothy sustained proved to be fatal.

His diaphragm was damaged, making the blood loss too much and his breathing was getting shallower by the second. Jeff's own wounds were painful as well; his entire back had been toasted and skin torn, but all he cared about at that moment was saving his friend and colleague.

By the time cavalry arrived, the enemy had retreated, and Timothy had died in Jeff's arms.

Later, he was told that the cavalry took time as, on the western side of Da Nang, the North Vietnamese had launched a rocket attack. It was Katyusha, a type of rocket artillery first built and fielded by the Soviet Union in World War II. Multiple rocket launchers such as these deliver explosives to a target area more intensively than conventional artillery. The ones that the Northern Vietnamese were using were 122mm unguided rockets with a 5-inch warhead. It destroyed anything it hit. His commander told him that they had feared this might be another attack of such type, and that's why the patrol team had taken a few minutes to respond.

After that first attack, this became a recurring incident as the enemies would use the Katyusha rocket launcher and fire for 15 minutes at them every week. This was 1972, and Major General Donald W. Reginald was commanding the 1st Marine Battalion, 2nd Battalion, and 389th Tactical Fighter Squadron. Along with the 366th Tactical Fighter Wing, he was a man with a mission and made sure they defended their base as well as Da Nang from PAVN/VC troops.

"I just want to see him one last time, and if that's not possible, then at least let me hear his voice .. . call the regiment or air base, ask them to make Jeffy boy call home . . . " Jeff's Grandfather broke into a fit of cough as he pleaded with Uncle Roger.

"I'm tryin', Pa; I've written a letter and have also called some friends to somehow make it known to Jeff that you're not well and wanna see him or talk to him."

"Try harder. I miss my boy. He's alive, right, Roger? Tell me nothin' happened to him!" Jeff's Grandfather demanded, his voice shaking.

"He's alright, Pa. I promise ya . . . my friend is also stationed in Vietnam; he sent a wire last week and told me that Jeff's doin' fine. He's in Da Nang and now 1Lt. He got promoted!" Roger told him proudly.

"Then ask your friend to make Jeff reach out to us."

"I'm tryin,' Pa, I'm tryin.' Now, you need to rest." Roger told his ailing father as Jeff's mother entered the room with some broth and medicine. As she tended to the old man, Roger looked at his father with worry evident on his face.

Two weeks after the attack, the I Corps went on red alert as they had gotten the intel that PAVN/VC was launching a full-fledged attack on all frontiers. The reconnaissance teams were assembled, and a defense strategy was devised to contain the enemy and not let them infiltrate the defensive zone. Initially, mortar shelling and 40mm rocket launchers were used by the enemy troops as they were seen carrying them along the western mountain ridge.

They hit the 1st Marine Battalion post but were deterred; however, as the day progressed, the artillerymen from both sides amped up their military response. The PAVC breached the 1st line of defense and launched a Katyusha 122mm MLR attack on their main base. After this, Jeff's squadron leader ordered a full-scale attack.

The hostilities carried on for 24 hours, during which both sides incurred heavy casualties. The I Corps lost some major bases but still managed to save their main base and push back the enemies. All in all, they managed to protect themselves from a hostile takeover, and eventually, the enemy retreated and conceded defeat. A ceasefire was agreed upon.

Jeff and his battalion also played a major role as they bombarded PAVN's main bases as well as shelter camps.

It was due to his skills that he was noticed.

Jeff was having breakfast one day when sergeant major hollered at him to join him immediately.

"I've heard you're a daredevil and a mighty fine pilot, Lt. Red," the sergeant major commented.

"I follow orders, sir, and rely on my survival instincts, so if that makes me a daredevil . . . " Jeff left the sentence unfinished and shrugged.

"Hmm . . . well, we are in a dilemma. This is sensitive information and a real precarious mission, one that only a seasoned pilot can do."

"What is it, sir?" Jeff asked.

"As you know, the hostilities have commenced for now, and we are in a state of ceasefire. There has been no exchange of gunfire, sneak attacks, MLR attacks or even mortar shelling . . . however," the sergeant major paused.

Jeff stood motionless, looking stoic as he waited for the man to continue.

"We have a special unit that has been working under the radar and has been providing intel. However, recently, those men have been cornered by the Northern Vietnamese and are trapped. They need to be rescued. And since these 63 special forces men have been a secret, we cannot ask for cavalry or any other allied group to help us in the rescue process," he explained.

"I see," Jeff replied.

"Yes, a special fighter aircraft needs to be used to rescue those men since no marine or ground route can be used."

"I see, and when do I leave?"

"As soon as possible. I'm banking on you, lieutenant. The lives of 63 of your colleagues hang in the balance. Please don't disappoint me."

Jeff knew the responsibility placed on him was huge, putting him in a precarious position. He knew he needed to be completely committed to the mission. He had thoroughly gone over all the plans and devised a strategy. He instructed the team to position their aircraft toward the runway and connect their power while he would go and rescue the guys.

It was a difficult task and a risky one, for this wasn't part of the protocol, but Jeff knew he had to try. So, he called the tower to ask permission to take off, but they refused.

"There's no way we can let you do this; it's a suicide mission and one that will put everyone at risk. You are not permitted," they responded.

"To heck with it!" Jeff swore and wondered if breaking the protocol would jeopardize his career and if he should back down. In the end, he decided otherwise. Cutting off the control tower, he took off without permission.

A responsibility had been placed on his shoulders, and come hell or high water, he was going to carry out the mission.

Risking It All

"It has been a horrible week. The Northerners have been a pain in the backside since last week," Captain Arnold Davy complained as he took a sip of his coffee.

"Be glad that it's a ceasefire today. At least we can enjoy our coffee in peace if nothing else," Master Sergeant Rick Andrews pointed out.

"Uhh ... sir, you need to come see this." Technical Sergeant Lewis Harper hurried toward the two men as they were sitting, enjoying their coffee.

"What's wrong? Have they breached the ceasefire?" Captain Davy asked, immediately alert.

"No, but perhaps we have," came the reply.

"What do you mean?" Sergeant Rick Andrews was perplexed.

"A 1Lt. is flying a fighter jet, despite the control tower not giving him the clear off," he quickly answered.

"That's preposterous; he can't do that. It's against protocols!" The captain exclaimed.

"Yes, sir. I was at the gangplank when I saw the fighter jet taxing. Then I heard that the control tower asked him to abort the mission."

"This doesn't make sense. Let's go and see what this is all about, Captain." Sergeant Rick stood up, and they all hurried toward the runway. As they made their way, they could see a lot of commotion and shouting, for the fighter plane had just jettisoned off toward the sky—the pilot was activating the afterburners after takeoff.

"Damn! Alert the Colonel in command now. This is gonna be a disaster!" Captain Davy swore, his expressions tinged with fear and anger.

The minute Jeff activated the afterburners after takeoff, the jet sped up as they were the additional combustion component used on some military jets, mostly those of military supersonic jets. The one Jeff was flying had these as this supersonic flight was important for combat and reconnaissance missions. Afterburning significantly increases thrust, and overtly increases the speed of the jet, eating up long distances fairly quickly.

As Jeff maneuvered the aircraft toward his destination, he was able to reach the area in under five minutes from the place where the special 63 were trapped within the enemy territory.

In military operations, different colored smokes are used to communicate critical information to other units, such as the location of friendly forces or the that of the enemy targets. The use of colored smoke can be an effective way to communicate in situations where traditional methods, such as radio communication, may be unavailable or unreliable. This was an SOP signal that was used to determine the location of either a stranded party waiting for rescue, a call for assistance, or to pinpoint the enemy's location. It acts as an alert signal. Various colored smoke grenades have no particular meaning as to color, with the possible exception that orange smoke is used in distress to mark one's location because it is the most visible from a distance. The various colors are used as a challenge/response when it is known or assumed that the enemy also has colored smoke.

While using colored smoke can be effective in certain situations, it is not without risks. If an enemy force has access to similar colored smoke, they may be able to use it to mislead or confuse friendly forces. Additionally, the use of colored smoke can draw attention to the location of friendly forces, potentially making them vulnerable to enemy fire.

To mitigate these risks, military personnel are trained to use colored smoke in conjunction with other communication methods and to be cautious about revealing their position.

In Vietnam, the USAF had learned the hard way. When the Viet Cong (the Communist guerrilla movement in Vietnam siding with the North Vietnamese Army against them) captured American smoke grenades, they would often light one off, hoping to lure a rescue mission for an ambush or to fool a base to allow their troops inside the perimeter.

Ever since then, Jeff and the rest of the battalion used caution. Sometimes, they wouldn't disclose the color until the last minute.

On this occasion, the smoke color of the day was blue. The enemy usually blows smoke of different colors to give away their position in the air so all the pilots know where they are. The Vietnamese were unaware of the color of the smoke that would reveal the precise location to the pilot, as Jeff's infantry changed the colors every day.

Nearing the location, he told the trapped men to blow the smoke to give away their position. When their smoke went up, Jeff saw a bunch of colors, red and orange, which were always around the blue smoke. He understood that both orange and red smoke signified danger, which meant these were the enemy lines, while the blue smoke indicated the location of the trapped 63.

Jeff hovered over the area, taking in the topography and hatching out a plan accordingly. Planning his route, he calculated an effective strategy of attack. Then he made a pass, dropping napalm down one side of the enemy, then the other, and then both ends, making a complete square around the pinned-down troops.

Jeff knew napalm would not only effectively damage the enemy lines but would also affect them psychologically. Napalm is an incendiary mixture of a gelling agent and a volatile petrochemical, such as gasoline (petrol) or diesel fuel. It was developed in a secret laboratory at Harvard in 1942 and then effectively used as a means of chemical warfare in the form of firebombing in World War II.

The reason napalm became so popular was because it burns at a high temperature and for longer times, unlike gasoline. Plus, it is comparatively easily dispersed and sticks to its targets. It is also deployable from both air and ground. During combustion, napalm generates large amounts of carbon monoxide and carbon dioxide.

In the Vietnam War, the use of napalm had become the most intrinsic element of U.S. military action against the enemy due to its tactical and psychological effects. Jeff had seen how napalm could destroy and kill barracks, towers, and enemy hideouts, all in a matter of minutes. Once he had dropped the napalm strategically and cleared the area, it was time to return to base.

Jeff's mother was working in the kitchen, making dinner and bone broth for her ailing father-in-law.

"Is the broth ready? He's feeling hungry, which is a good sign, I suppose," Uncle Roger asked as he entered the kitchen.

"Yes, just about." She nodded and started filling up the bowl with the broth. "You'll be staying for dinner?" she turned to hand him the tray.

"Nah, Jenny's home alone as the farm boy took off to visit his family."

"How's Jenny?" she asked.

"She's well . . . how are you holdin' up? Has he raised his hand on you again?" he asked.

"Under the circumstances, I'm doin' fine. And no, he's been busy, lookin' after the farm and worryin' about the money. He's rarely ever home."

"What about Pa? Ain't he worried about him? He's his father, too."

"He is, but then again, all he shows is anger and frustration, so I don't know if he's worried or not. D'ya know in all the time Jeff has been gone, he hasn't asked about his son even once," she told him tearfully.

"I will never understand why he has this beef with his own son. It simply makes no sense." Roger shook his head.

"Any word from Jeff?"

"I'm tryin' . . . hopefully, we'll hear from him soon." He tried to assure her.

"Amen." She nodded, then turned away.

As the plane landed and taxied on the runway, Jeff could see a crowd awaiting him. He knew he was in trouble and was going to get quite an earful for what he had done.

He got out of the aircraft and made his way toward the main building, but he was intercepted.

"What were you thinking, you idiot?" The Colonel in command yelled as Jeff approached him. He gave the man a salute and remained silent in return.

"Were you given a clearance for flying, lieutenant?" Captain Davy asked.

"No, sir," he replied.

"Then what in God's name propelled you to go on a firebombing mission on a ceasefire day?" Captain Davy inquired angrily.

"It was a covert mission, sir."

"Covert mission, my foot. I think you've got a taste for killing, young man. I know they call you ace because you've shot down more than five enemy aircraft in aerial combat. I read your file; you've brutally injured enemies in hand-to-hand combat, and recently, your junior died in your arms. Perhaps that has done you in. You've lost your marbles and need a psych evaluation," the Colonel stated.

"I'm perfectly alright, sir. I was given a mission that I carried out perfectly. I don't have anything else to say on that," Jeff replied stoically.

"Well, I have a lot to say on the matter. You can't just ignore the orders of your superiors and do as you please. There are protocols to follow that can't be ignored. Military is all about the discipline you've breached, and you shall be punished for it!" the Colonel spoke vehemently.

"The Colonel is right, lieutenant. What you've done is highly irresponsible and risky. It also defied the ceasefire, which will most likely result in an escalation of hostilities," Captain Davy added.

"Precisely, that's why I believe he should be imposed with Article 15. A demotion and a pay cut should teach him a lesson," the Commander Chief declared, making others gasp as they looked at Jeff. Even Jeff got worried as Article 15 is a military justice option that allows a commanding officer to decide the fate of an officer/soldier's innocence or guilt and administer the punishment, accordingly, depending on the nature of the offense under the Uniform Code of Military Justice (UCMJ)12345.

It's not a judicial proceeding or a trial but a proceeding that could determine a de-ranking, demotion, or pay cut of the said individual. It doesn't go up to court or legal proceedings, unlike a court martial.

Jeff knew Article 15 would be a blemish on his record, so he tried to reason.

"Sir, I was given official instructions, and the mission was important. Otherwise, I would have followed orders."

"I don't want to hear another thing. You will be informed of our decision; now, you may leave." The Colonel raised his hand and stopped Jeff from arguing further. Jeff knew the man was being unreasonable and was determined to deprive him of his lieutenant rank.

He looked at the implacable expressions of the men staring at him and cursed them inwardly. He finally raised his chin, saluted them, and made his way inside, seething at being subjected to this humiliation.

The Medal of Honor

That entire night, Jeff tossed and turned in bed. After the threat of Article 15, he had stalked back to his lodgings and stayed inside. He'd avoided going to dinner, and later, another lieutenant had brought him some food. He spent his time getting a little worked up and agitated, and only to distract himself, he re-read all the letters he'd received from home. Weirdly, though, he hadn't received a single letter in the past two months.

On this thought, Jeff decided to write a letter back home. He was a little worried about Gramps. In her last letter, his mother had written that Gramps was ill and had caught pneumonia in the winter, which left him bedridden. Jeff wanted to know how he was doing now.

He also wanted to enquire about his younger sister and brother and how they were holding up. Jesse was seven years younger than Jeff, and when he left home, she was just eleven years old, studying in middle school at the time. Meanwhile, Joey was ten years younger than him, and Jeff missed his baby brother. He remembered when he was born, he used to take care of him so that his mother could sleep in for a few hours and also do chores around the house uninterrupted.

While Jesse helped their mother with house chores, she was so young herself when Joey was born. As he grew up, he used to shadow Jeff everywhere. He had promised himself that he wouldn't let Pa beat 'em up the way he beat up Jeff. He protected his siblings, though sometimes, he couldn't reach them in time.

Jeff made his Uncle Roger promise him that he would look after Jeff's siblings in his absence. He was really glad when his Uncle had written to tell him that Joey was regularly going to the local school and also helping around the farm.

He reminisced about the old times as he finished writing the letter. He told his family about his accomplishments and the rescue mission he had just operated. He also told them about Vietnamese culture and then asked about every family member except for his father. What was the point? Then he inserted some money in the envelope before sealing it. He was also going to make a money order to send money home, as he had been saving for a while.

Afterward, as he lay on the bed, he thought about how unjust it was to threaten him with Article 15. He was angry at being treated the way he had been. Eventually, he fell asleep, but his dreams were dark, and the entire night was spent feeling restless.

Jeff woke up early the next morning, got dressed, and went for a run. He had so much pent-up energy that he needed to release it. Besides, he wanted to be done with his morning workout so as to get breakfast, as he was famished. Again, he wanted to avoid the crowds.

He made his way to the breakfast and got hot porridge, along with bacon and fried eggs, and then dug into the food.

"Yesterday was quite the heroics," 1Lt. Adam sat opposite him, a smirk playing on his lips.

"Leave me alone."

"Now, now, don't be so rude . . . I was just giving a compliment."

"Yeah, right!" Jeff grimaced, shoveling more food into his mouth. He and Adam were good friends, but the man was anything but diplomatic. And his blunt opinions sometimes irritated the hell out of Jeff, although he, himself, was quite straightforward.

"What do you want, Adam? Can't you lemme eat in peace?" Jeff asked.

"Course' I can, but then where would be the fun in that? Heard you got quite an earful and a threat of being Article 15 by the Colonel?"

"Yeah!"

"Well, that was quite some bravado, especially on a ceasefire day."

"Ohh, come off it. The enemy wasn't honoring it either. They kept shooting at the airbase and on our special convoys," Jeff countered.

"Fair enough, but you know how these men think. They want to make an example out of you, and they will do that."

"Yeah, I know."

"Aren't you worried?"

"Honestly, damn it. I saved all these men, and that man wants to bust me. I don't care if it was a ceasefire day; I did a run to save the lives of my brothers in war. So, nah, I'm not worried; pissed would be the right choice of word. Now, I'll eat my meal, have a recon of the weather, go through the flight schedule, and then see what the day brings," Jeff told him firmly, putting an end to the conversation.

Adam gave him a long look, then quietly focused on his own food, an uneasy silence descending between the two.

"There's not much that can be done. All you can do now is to keep him as warm and comfortable as possible. The constant coughing has damaged the elasticity of his lungs," the doctor told Roger as they stepped out to discuss Jeff's Grandfather's deteriorating health.

"How much time has he got?" Roger asked.

"Not a lot; the fluid accumulation in his lungs has exceeded. It can be a few weeks or 2-3 months. Can't give you a definitive answer," the doctor concluded.

Roger nodded, sadness washing over him. After seeing the doctor off, he stood on the porch with his hands jammed in his pocket and mouth pressed in a thin line.

"Grandpa is dying, isn't he, Uncle Roger?" Joey came to stand beside him; sweat beaded on his face since he had just returned from working in the fields. After school, he tended to help his father around the farm. The boy had grown up so much over time, and he reminded Roger so much of Jeff.

"Why'd you say that?"

"I heard you and Doc talkin'."

"I suppose there's no point in hiding it from you then. Yeah, Pa ain't gonna make it," Roger said gruffly.

"I wish Jeff was here. Grandpa really misses him, and so do we all," Joey shrugged.

"Yeah, if only . . . " Roger left the sentence unfinished. Wishing Jeff was with them was just that, wishful thinking. He hadn't seen the boy in years and had only spoken to him a handful of times.

"Pa is hopeful that this time, the corn production would be in surplus," Joey told him.

"I'm glad. Somethin' to look forward to," Roger nodded, his eyes settling on the horizon.

Jeff was surveying the weather report of the day that forecasted light rain later in the day, which roughly translated to quite a downpour since Vietnamese weather was rather unpredictable. In the beginning, Jeff had underestimated the weather and gotten stuck in torrential downpours. He still remembered navigating the plane through extreme weather, with the threat of lightning bolts toasting the plane. Luckily, he had been able to make an emergency landing.

The sound of rotor blades in the air broke his reverie. He looked outside on the landing dock, and there, a CH-47 Chinook was taxiing. The Chinook helicopter was especially made to the requirements of the U.S. Army. They performed various transport missions, transporting troops, war supplies, and battlefield equipment. The helicopter could also be deployed in medical evacuation, search and rescue, aircraft recovery, parachute drop, and other operations.

Curiosity made him focus on the personnel getting out of the Chinook, but just then, Captain Davy came in and asked Jeff to follow him.

They both entered Colonel's office, where he was sitting behind the desk, talking on the phone.

"Why weren't we informed about this before? It should have been mentioned that they will be coming to our base."

"I see, very well." He grimaced as he listened to the person on the phone, then angrily put the phone down.

"Yes, Captain Davy, what is it?" The Colonel asked in irritation.

"You wanted to see him," Captain Davy gestured toward Jeff.

"I just wanted you to know, lieutenant, that for now, you're not to leave the base or take on any flights today. Till we finalize Article 15, you are to remain in your barracks," the Colonel dismissed Jeff.

"This is unfair. I did what I had to do to save the lives of my countrymen!" Jeff argued.

"Do not dig your grave any further. Now please leave."

Captain Davy motioned Jeff to remain silent and leave. With fists clenched on his side, Jeff had no other choice but to walk out in silence.

While Jeff had been in his barracks, 63 special forces arrived in Da Nang. These men were carrying fishhooks on their sides, and one ear from each of Jeff's kills that saved them hung from the hooks. The ears were of 563 Vietnamese who had ambushed and surrounded them.

These men were the special forces that were Jeff's covert mission. Their Sergeant Major had arrived along with some other personnel in the Chinook. The Sergeant inquired about the whereabouts of Lieutenant Red, as that was Jeff's call sign.

Jeff's comrades were a little perplexed as to why someone so important was asking about a 1Lt.

"Perhaps he's come here to discuss Article 15. Although it sounds a little farfetched," An Lt2 speculated.

Nevertheless, they pointed to Jeff's barracks—a makeshift tent hut. The special forces strode toward the barracks and called Jeff before entering.

"Lieutenant Red, we've been looking for you all over," their Sergeant said as other men joined him in the cramped space. The Sergeant stepped forward and kissed Jeff right on the lips.

"Thank you so much for saving my men. I'm proud of you! Look at my boots; they were partly melted from your fire spreading, but that was the only damage," he told Jeff.

"Look, we got you souvenirs as a thank you gift," one of the special forces men said, and they raised their fishing hooks, ears dangling from the rods.

Jeff was speechless and a little amazed at this gesture.

"I'm glad y'all are okay. Rescuing was my patriotic duty, sir," Jeff said once he found his voice.

"I think the space is too cramped. Let's step outside," someone suggested, and they stepped outside the barracks.

The Sergeant Major who sent Jeff was already walking toward the barracks, and as he came near, he began hugging the special forces one by one.

"I heard y'all arrived in Da Nang and were at the base, so I came out to meet everyone. So, glad to see y'all," he told them.

"I really appreciate you sending this young man for the rescue mission and also for calling me about the other thing," the Sergeant spoke.

"What in the name is happening here?" the Colonel in Command demanded as Captain Davy accompanied him.

"What does it look like? We're greeting the man who saved our backs," the special forces Sergeant smirked.

"I don't understand," he said.

"I heard your skirmish yesterday when you were reprimanding 1Lt. Jeff, and since I was the one who sent him on the mission as per the Major's request, I thought calling him here was the best course of action," Sergeant Major explained.

"I see; well, it's good that everyone's here. I came out to announce that I am stripping the lieutenant of his rank," Colonel declared.

Hearing these words, all 63 men raised their guns and trained them on the Colonel, who was pissed.

"Hold it, the General is coming. He'll sort this out," Sergeant Major told them.

"Good morning," the General arrived. He was quite an impressive personality, with a commanding air about him.

"You must be the Colonel in Command. I'm General Richards," he introduced himself, and both men shook hands.

"So, pray tell, Colonel, why are you de-ranking 1Lt. Jeff?" the General demanded.

"Because he disobeyed a direct order not to take off on a ceasefire day," Colonel responded.

"But since the enemy was shooting at all the special forces, we figured it was just another day. It wasn't really a ceasefire," the Sergeant Major told the Colonel.

"Doesn't matter; he breached protocol that showed a lack of discipline. He deserves Article 15," Colonel argued.

"I don't think so, Colonel. I believe Lieutenant Jeff truly showed great discipline, presence of mind, and courage. And for that reason, even though he may have disobeyed a direct order, he saved 63 special forces men and killed 563 of the enemy. I'm putting his name forward for Medal of Honor," the General declared.

Jeff looked at the General with shock, not believing his ears, whereas the Colonel got red in the face.

"I can't let you do that!" he bellowed.

"Excuse me! You do realize that I outrank you? And given I've told you the lieutenant would not be stripped of his rank or face Article 15; my decision is final. He will instead be named for the medal," the General stated firmly.

"Sir, with all due respect. I really think this is not a wise decision, and the lieutenant answers to me," Colonel protested.

"He answers to the United States, and he served the United States! As for not making a wise decision, let me make a wise one that would benefit all. You are being stripped of your rank as Colonel. You will face Article 15 in response to repeatedly questioning my judgment," The General announced amidst shocked gasps around him, as no one was expecting this twist, especially Jeff.

That day, the Colonel was given Jeff's Article 15 from the General, and his rank was stripped to Major.

Going Down

◆━━━━━━━●━━━━━━━◆

"I'm sorry . . . he's no more," the doctor told Roger as he recorded the time of death and pronounced Jeff's Grandfather dead. They had shifted him to the nearest hospital when his condition worsened, and they could no longer make him comfortable at home.

Until his last breath, the dying man had called for Jeff repeatedly, but alas, they couldn't contact the boy; although they had received his letter and the money order. It was apparent from the contents of his letter that he didn't know the gravity of Pa's situation. And now it was too late, for in the past two weeks, Roger's father's health had deteriorated badly, and no amount of care could bring comfort to the man.

"When can we take the body home? I need to make funeral arrangements accordingly," Roger asked the doctor, and then they commenced discussing the formalities, whereas Jeff's father remained stoic, standing at the corner of the room, his face impassive.

"I still can't believe the Colonel got Article 15 instead of you—quite the plot twist, mate," 1Lt. Adam smacked Jeff on his shoulder as the two men reviewed their flight plan for the day.

"Yeah, well, he deserved it," Jeff shrugged.

"Hmm, and congrats on the nomination for the Medal of Honor. That's big, dude. You've become quite a legend among the juniors!"

"Thanks, I guess."

"Here you go, lieutenant; sorry your mail got mixed up with mine, and it took me a while to realize it," said another 1Lt. sharing the same name as he handed Jeff a pile of letters.

"Oh, no wonder I haven't been receiving any mail lately," Jeff said as he went through the pile.

Later in the day, once he was done with his reconnaissance flight and had returned to the base, Jeff settled into his barracks and started reading the letters. As he went through them, his expression changed from worry to panic; the last letter making him dash for the radio room.

"Uncle Roger, it's me, Jeff . . . how's Gramps?" Jeff asked over the phone.

"Jeff, is that you? I can't hear you!" Roger shouted on the other end.

"You're breaking up. I just got the letters that Gramps isn't well. How is he?" Jeff asked.

"You're too late, Jeff. Your Gramps is no more. He died," Roger told him.

"No . . . that can't be!" Jeff yelled.

"He really wanted to see you or hear your voice. We tried to get a call through so many times, but it never worked. I'm sorry."

"I didn't know what was going on. The base was attacked a while ago . . . so that's why, I think. I just can't believe it about Gramps. I . . . " Jeff's voice trailed off as grief assailed him.

He had to go through so much red tape to have this phone call home, and hearing the news totally broke him. He loved his Grandfather, and to hear that the man wasn't alive anymore and that he would never get to see him or hear him was heartbreaking.

"Your Grandfather may be gone, but just know this, Jeffy boy, he was so proud of you. Don't beat yourself up. We love you and miss you," Roger emphasized the last words, knowing how hard the news was for his nephew.

Sometimes, the grief was too overwhelming for Jeff. Losing his Grandfather and not being able to say the last goodbye gutted him. He had channeled all that grief and sorrow in his work and taken on more assignments just to put the dark thoughts at bay.

He had called his mother as well, who was also broken by the news. His Gramps had been her major support and like a fatherly figure. The family was heartbroken, and they wanted Jeff to come home, but Jeff knew it was impossible. They were in the middle of a war. So, he had no option but to process his loss on his own.

That day, as usual, Jeff did a recon of the weather and checked his flight plan, as well as his oil gauge and engine, before preparing for the flight. The weather was sunny, and it was a routine mission.

He was about 15 miles from Da Nang on a routine bombing mission, flying low to make the exact hits where the North Vietnamese ground troops were. They started firing and got lucky as one of the shells went through the fuel tank and landed in Jeff's right knee. It felt like a bee sting. As Jeff looked out, he saw the left engine was on fire. It was engulfed in flames, and he was too close to the ground.

He turned it straight up and climbed as fast as he could, trying to get altitude to parachute out since altitude was required for that. While powering up, it was apparent that the engine and tank were about to blow the speed to nearly 400mph or more; too fast, but Jeff had to eject anyway.

Jeff had sent a mayday out to his position and radioed to get help. Luckily, he was over familiar territory and knew where he would be. The explosion of the plane landing about two miles away from the enemy territory was sure to find him near the Northern Vietnamese army. While the plane was nosing down, the seat straps on the plane seat tightened down so much that he could not break loose. He tried to loosen it but could not get out of the seat and prepared for the impact.

Jeff hit the ground so hard it shattered his L5. And when he looked down, blood was running down the leg where he had been shot in the knee. He was in immense pain. His lumbar spine seemed to be on fire, pain ricocheting throughout his body. The ejection from the plane and landing at 25mph had caused the lower back injury. Wincing from the effort, Jeff cut the straps loose, got out of the seat, crawled over to a tree, and leaned on it. Dragging himself took herculean effort, and in retrospect, had it not been an adrenaline rush and the need to save himself, Jeff would never have been able to get out, given the seriousness of his injury.

All the while, Jeff prayed to get rescued, as he knew the enemy would soon descend on him. He was hoping that the special forces unit he had rescued heard his distress call and were inside a helicopter, rushing toward him as soon as possible.

As he leaned on the tree and looked around, he told himself that there was no way he would allow himself to be captured, as the Vietnamese were known for their animalistic treatment. They would take the officers and pilots and drive bamboo under their fingernails and toenails. Then, they resorted to peeling one raw with a knife to create pain in hopes of extracting information from their captive. Jeff had seen a pilot who had gone through an hour of that punishment. His battalion had to order a hit from a sniper to put that pilot out of his misery. Jeff shuddered as he thought of it.

He checked his 45-cal pistol, which had two clips, eight rounds each, as he knew they must have seen him going down. He knew it was only a matter of time before they found him, and one thing he knew for sure was that he would not let them take him alive.

It took about 20 minutes for the enemy to circle him, and sure enough, after he had made a tourniquet for his knee, they started showing up one by one until they spotted him. One of them started closing in on him, so Jeff shot him. He took the shots very carefully, killing them one at a time. He saved the last two shells for himself, as the 45 was known for its misfiring. Jeff started to pray to God for forgiveness as he knew committing suicide was a sin, and he did not want to kill himself, but before going through the torture at their hands, Jeff preferred to end his life by his own hands.

At that moment, he thought of his family—his mother, siblings, and Uncle. Thinking of them made his eyes glisten with tears. There was so much he wanted to say to them. He ached to see them, but here he was, so far away from home in a country where he knew no one, and stuck in a forest with his enemies closing in on him. Life flashed before his eyes as he prayed to God and then lifted the gun to put it to the side of his head. He pulled the hammer back and squeezed the trigger. He choked out, "I'm sorry, Ma ... "

Just then, he felt the gun being pushed up, skimming the top of his head and blowing out his eardrum.

"Are you crazy?" someone yelled.

In his pain, confusion, and state of fear, Jeff hadn't heard the approaching helicopter. He was so hyper focused on avoiding capture that when a sergeant dived and pushed the gun up in the air just as it went off, Jeff was startled. The man had saved his life!

It appeared that the special forces had arrived about 23 minutes after Jeff had ejected and called for help. He was told that they got as close as they could and started to run, and the sergeant dived to save Jeff from killing himself just in the nick of time. The medic attended to him while the special forces men took care of the enemy. Upon survey, they gathered that there were about 25 of the enemy still trying to get to Jeff, and the eight special forces took M148 grenade launchers mounted on their M16s and killed all of them.

The helicopter landed about 100 yards away, and they had him on a stretcher, with two carrying Jeff and six shooting at another patrol that was headed that way. As the men carried him toward the helicopter, the constant jolting and ducking worsened the pain in his back. The roar of the chopper blades, as well as the continuous shelling, made Jeff feel like his head would explode. To him, every second counted, and there was a moment where Jeff feared they would never be able to make it to the chopper, for the enemy fire was so constant.

However, the special forces had two other helicopters, with eight men in each, that came quickly to their rescue and started firing and killing a lot of the enemy that were upon them. Incidentally, Jeff had shot 13 Vietnamese with his 45, and the special forces had killed about 30 to 40 of the Vietnamese and stopped the attacks on them completely until they were flying home.

However, while they were carrying him back to safety, one of the helicopters above them took a hit and started spiraling down to the ground and exploded, killing the pilot and one crew member manning the 50 calypter machine gun. Also, when they were airborne, one of the men took a shot in the chest from a lucky shot from the Vietnamese on the ground.

The rescue mission was precarious, and it took them a while to get back to base. Jeff's injuries were not life threatening but severe, and he was glad to be alive and on his way back to Da Nang without a loss of a limb. In those moments between his plane crash and his rescue, when fear had taken root and death had loomed over him, Jeff realized just how precious life really was.

The Bar Trip

Lying on the infirmary bed, Jeff winced as pain shot up in his back and traveled through his lower abdomen all the way to his banged-up leg. He clenched his jaw and groaned, the pain making his eyes water.

When he'd been rescued and brought back to the base, the resident doctor had checked his injuries and ordered him to be taken to the infirmary. Jeff's lumbar injury was serious, and although he had stopped the blood loss when he was shot, he had developed an infection, which left him delirious with a fever. He was told that he would be down for 30 days and wouldn't be able to fly for the next six weeks.

Jeff wished he could have avenged himself. He knew the base would, but they could not act on aggression very much as there was no one to go against since they all were very isolated. And there wasn't any point, really. They had the opportunity, which they capitalized on. He was lucky that he was saved.

Initially, the pain and fever had made him not care about this much, but as time passed, he felt frustrated. Lying in the bed, Jeff was left to his own devices, which meant often reminiscing about home and his Gramps. He still couldn't believe that his Grandfather was no more and had a hard time accepting that whenever he would go home, he wouldn't find him there.

A fleeting memory of the day Jeff was leaving for training assuaged him.

Gramps was waiting for Jeff to say his goodbyes to the family, and once he had bid everyone farewell, Uncle Roger was going to take him to the station. Gramps wasn't well enough to ride along with them, so he walked with Jeff until the end of the dirt path.

"Make me proud, boy, and remember when in doubt or a tough situation, this old man will be praying for you," he told Jeff.

"I'm gonna miss you, Gramps," Jeff said tearfully.

"Me too, boy, but you've chosen your path. May God be with you," Gramps hugged him, and with one final lingering look, Jeff turned and walked toward the waiting car. Gramps remained standing, looking at the car driving away until it rounded the bend. Only then did Jeff turn around in his seat and look forward. This was the last memory Jeff had of his Grandfather.

A solitary tear slid down his cheek as he lay there, thinking of his late Grandfather and the family he had left behind.

"The Viet Cong and Northerners have joined forces against the South Vietnamese Army. Two Americans were killed and 41 wounded, including four women and five children, when a VC bomb was set off in a sports stadium during a softball game. There was a second bomb as well, but it failed to explode," Captain Davy reported to the

Commander Sergeant, as the Airforce officials and dignitaries, along with the U.S. Marines and Military personnel, sat around the round table, looking at the reports laid out in front of them.

"Were there any locals among the injured or just the Americans?" the sergeant asked.

"A few locals also died, but since the softball match was primarily arranged by the consulate, most of the wounded were our fellow Americans," he explained.

"Very well, what about the bombardment our fighter jets did on the village they were hiding in?" one of the colonels asked.

"That was a trap, sir, just like in the past. Due to the VC's scheming and the Northern Army's ransacking of American settlements, our hasty reaction or retaliatory attacks on villagers through sniping, raids, or placing mines and booby traps in and near villages left a negative impression on the local populace. So, when our soldiers were captured near that village and then killed, the Northern Army entered the village and harangued the local populace about supporting the Revolution before digging in and passing word to the district capital that they were active in the community. They were insinuating that the villagers were involved with them," Captain Davy paused, taking in the silence in the room.

"Well, the next day, U.S. planes bombed the village and its Catholic church. VC operatives emerged after the destruction to tell survivors about the duplicity of the U.S. Army, calling us imperialists and oppressors."

"So, our retaliatory attack was a misjudgment?" the sergeant asked.

"To an extent, yes, which makes it imperative that we fight this propaganda forming against us. The local sentiment can't be volatile toward us," the captain concluded.

"I concur. We need to be more careful, especially when it comes to gathering intelligence and reconnaissance missions," the sergeant agreed.

"Hmm, but what about the bombing attacks that the VC and Northerners have regularly started? Just two weeks ago, a bomb exploded in front of the Hung Dao Hotel, Saigon, a guesthouse for American servicemen, that injured eight Vietnamese and three Americans who were in the street at the time.

Moreover, the VC threw a grenade into a Da Nang home where an American family was having dinner, killing a French businessman and wounding four other persons. These people are getting vicious," said the Chief Commander of the Marines Corp, his expressions thunderous.

"Caution! That's the only thing that can be practiced because retaliation under provocation further complicates things," the sergeant suggested.

Later that day, after the briefing, a memo was passed around to remain alert and cautious, as well as instructions to be vigilant when doing reconnaissance missions.

"How are you, Ma? How's everyone back at home?" Jeff spoke on the phone. He was finally out of the infirmary and could walk and do light exercises again. Currently, he was at the control tower, calling home.

"I'm better, and so is everyone else. Your siblings are doing fine. You know, your sister is going to finish high school soon," she told him.

"I'm glad to hear it. How's Uncle Roger?" he asked.

"He's fine. Your aunt is expecting. The new baby is due soon. What about you? In your letter, you told me about the injuries you sustained during a mission," she sounded worried.

"I'm recovering now. The doctor has given me the clear, but it'll still be two weeks before I can fly again."

"Jeff, your father is getting older; managing the farm is becoming difficult for him," she hesitated as she said these words.

"Then hire help, Ma."

"Why don't you come back home, Jeff? Your Gramps is gone, and your father is ailing. I'm here all alone," she pleaded.

"You know I can't leave, not until my assignment finishes. Besides, I'm the one alone here. You've got both Jesse and Joey with you as well as Pa and Uncle … " he trailed off.

"But I want my son back. The fear of losing you doesn't let me sleep at night. It's been ages since I last saw you," she cried.

"Don't cry, Ma. Just pray for me that I get back home safely. Gotta go now, I'll call again." Jeff finished the call, feeling a little upset.

He ambled toward the stairway, slowly making his way to the gymnasium for some exercise.

Jeff and his comrades decided to head into town to celebrate his return to duty but also to say farewell to a buddy of his who was going back home in three days.

They had been in town a couple of times, but that day, the plan was to visit the bar where they served the special Vietnamese rice wine and Bia hơi or Bia tươi, which was a type of draught beer popular in Vietnam. It was often served in street corner bars.

Jeff liked the flavor and was also looking forward to eating some good calamari and Pho, which was noodle soup. He had been to the bar a couple of times, and since it wasn't a local haunt, the boys didn't feel too out of place there. In fact, the owner spoke English and was always friendly toward them.

While the others took their seat and placed their orders, Jeff went over to the old jukebox at the back of the bar and put a coin in to play a song of his liking.

"Man, I'm so jealous of you right now. You get to fly away from this hellhole and be back home with your people, whereas we're still stuck here in this forsaken country," a fellow officer whined.

"Hey! I was posted here before y'all were, and I've paid my dues; now skedaddle," Brad, who was the officer leaving for home, smirked.

Just then, their drinks and food arrived, and Jeff raised his bottle to Brad.

"To Brad, for going back home. Have a safe journey, dude," he toasted, and everyone joined in.

They all dug into the food, Jeff reveling in the first bite of Pho and fried calamari. They all bantered with each other, sharing lewd jokes and teasing Brad about his girlfriend, who was waiting back at home. This made the man blush.

Once they were done with food, they ordered another round of drinks, and now the conversation turned serious. There were about 20 servicemen, all sitting around a round table. Jeff looked at some of them who had recently joined the ranks and still had a hint of youth left in them. Meanwhile, some's faces had hardened with time and the traumas they suffered during the war.

Jeff himself felt weariness seep into him.

"The VC executed two wounded American prisoners of war near the village of An Châu. Their hands were tied, and they both were shot in the face because one could not keep up with the retreating captors. And then they decided to kill the other one too," a serviceman grimaced as he told them about the latest atrocities committed by the enemy.

"They be damned, I'm so sick of their barbaric behavior," Jeff said, shaking his head.

"Yeah, I just want this to be over now. We've been issued the memo to watch our back. But that's what we've been doing since the beginning," another chimed in.

In his peripheral vision, Jeff saw a young child of 8-9 years entering the bar with an older man, probably her father. He wasn't surprised to see this, as the drinking culture was pretty prevalent in Vietnam, and children tagging along with their parents to bars wasn't that unusual.

The girl looked at them and started smiling, getting excited. She said, "Hug G.I., hug G.I." This made them laugh as they were a little taken aback to think she knew of G.I. Joe and thought of them as one. Some of them waved at her, but the girl kept chanting, "Hug G.I. . . ."

A young army man approached her and bent down to hug her. He squatted to eye level and smiled at her. Jeff saw her father inching away and standing at the far corner of the bar. He thought it was weird.

One of the service members noticed the pins from a grenade popping out under the girl's arm; he then looked with horror at his colleague who was hugging the girl. In an instant, the Sergeant sitting next to Jeff dived on top of him, three others following quickly to contain the blast.

All Jeff heard was a loud explosion, a deafening noise. Shrapnel hit him in the arm, causing searing pain and utter chaos. He felt suffocated under the weight of the bodies and could barely see anything as smoke clouded his vision. The smell of things burning around him and screams further disoriented him.

That day, five U.S. soldiers were killed, and around 10 of the servicemen were severely injured. Jeff was hit in the arm, and the Sergeant who jumped was heavily wounded on his side and back.

Brad was among the men who died; the girl killed him as he was one of the men right by her side when she popped the pins.

Once again, Jeff had escaped death thanks to his fellow officers. But he was devastated for Brad, who was ecstatic to go home. Now, his remains, wrapped in the American flag, would be transported back to his land.

While the U.S. government condemned the attack, there was nothing that could be done. There were a few suicide attacks, and the government would not even investigate them as they knew the Vietnamese talked young children into committing these acts, either by forcing them or giving incentives to their poverty-stricken families.

The children were collateral damage in this ugly war.

The White House

The aftermath of the suicide bombing was horrific; the smell of blood and gore, paired with burning flesh, still made Jeff wretch whenever he remembered it. Although his colleagues had saved him, all of them had sustained burns and cuts. Their injuries were severe enough that most of them were transferred to Saigon to get better treatment and a psych evaluation.

Jeff was already recovering from his previous injuries when he once again got injured during the blast, resulting in burns this time around. The deceased were taken to Saigon, so he never got the chance to attend the funeral services of his comrades.

He remained in Saigon for a couple of weeks to recover from his injuries as, once again, flying was out of the question. While the injured were convalescing, they'd found out two more such attacks were carried out, one on the convoy traveling outside of Da Nang and another on the battalion that was out in the town.

This was also the time when Washington realized, despite their military and technological advancements, they were fighting a losing battle because their advanced weapons were ineffective against a country that was not industrialized and an army that employed guerrilla tactics, using the dense jungle as cover.

Indeed, the North Vietnamese army's way of fighting was conventional, orthodox, and effective, for they knew their land more than the Americans. Kidnapping, maiming, bomb blasts, minefield explosions, and suicide bombings were their way of defeating the U.S..

Jeff and his fellow comrades knew that the U.S. hadn't gained any traction during this time, and the war was coming to a fold, so he wondered whether he would still be stationed here or would be shipped elsewhere. He hoped he wouldn't have to go back to Da Nang as he was done with that place.

However, soon, orders came, and Jeff and most of his comrades were being shipped back home since it seemed the Vietnam war was in its conclusive stage as President Nixon was mulling over it. It was soon after this that the North Vietnamese forces triggered a major offensive in the Central Highlands in March 1975. They had, by now, upgraded their logistics system and rebuilt their forces, as well as acquired advanced weaponry from the Soviet Union and China, who were backing them in the conflict. So, on April 30, 1975, NVA tanks moved through the gate of the Presidential Palace in Saigon, barging in and effectively ending the war.

The loss was bitter, but finally, a long and torturous war had come to an end. Many lives were lost in the process, and families were destroyed, but mercifully, Jeff had survived it and was happy to be going back home. The morale of the troops had been down because nobody liked waging a war and coming out on the wrong side of it. But perhaps this was an important lesson as well.

Jeff was shipped back to Minot, North Dakota, where he spent a week. Coming back to the States after spending years in the jungles of Vietnam was a surreal experience. The rolling hills, wide vistas, and suburban streets that greeted his sight were a huge welcome for Jeff. He had survived the war and was back in his land with only bumps and scrapes to show for it. Boy, was he glad!

Minot, North Dakota, is known for being home to Minot Air Force Base. The city's rich aviation history was told to all of them during their time there. The war veterans were debriefed at the air base before they were to be shipped out.

While there, Jeff explored the town a little and was impressed by the Scandinavian architecture of the buildings. There was a Scandinavian Heritage Park as well, honoring the city's rich immigrant history. He really relished them.

He savored the 180-degree change from hot and humid Vietnam to the chilly mornings and evenings of North Dakota.

A week later, he was released and went home to Lewisburg, Tennessee. The ride back home was uneventful, but Jeff was lost in the familiar scenery and the emotions that assailed him. He had left his home as a boy and was now coming back as a man who had seen too much loss and blood. The landscape hadn't changed, but everything else had.

No one was going to be there to greet him, nor would he be going to his farm and original homestead as his parents had sold the farm and moved into the city. In her letter, his mother had told him that, since the farm was not faring well, they had eventually decided to sell it, and the old man had gotten a job as a factory supervisor.

Reaching his new house, he hesitated going inside. Although he had informed his mother before coming that he would be home soon, he was still contemplating the situation when the door flew upon.

"You wanna spend an eternity on the doorstep?" the girl cocked an eyebrow and smirked.

"Uhh . . . Jesse?" Jeff looked at his grown-up sister.

"Who else, big brother? Wow, you've . . . big and a little mean-lookin'," she teased.

"So have you . . . I can't believe I'm seeing you after all these years," he gushed.

"Same, there was a point when we thought we wouldn't ever see you again . . ." She looked away as her voice trailed off.

Jeff nodded, swallowing a lump in his throat, and Jesse moved aside to let him in.

"Look, Ma. He's home," she called out to their mother. At that exact moment, she appeared, wiping her hands on her apron and beaming at Jeff. The years had taken its toll on her, and she looked frail but still beautiful, just like he remembered.

"Jeffy . . . oh my boy . . . " she hugged him, her voice brimming with emotions.

"Ma, how are you?" Jeff hugged her back, then gave her a searching look.

"I'm good, especially now that you're here. Go get some rest, Jesse, and show your brother his room. Dinner will be ready soon."

"Sure."

"Where's Joey and him?" he refused to call his father 'Pa.'

"Joey works at the local diner, so he'll be back late, and your dad's out . . . " She fidgeted with her apron, which was a telltale sign that she was avoiding answering him.

"He's at some watering hole, right? Drowning himself in a booze bottle?" Jeff asked, disgusted.

"Now, don't be pickin' fights with your Pa unnecessarily. He can't leave the bottle, and I'm fine with it, so just let it go," his mother pleaded, and Jeff gave a long sigh. He knew it was too much to hope that his father would have sobered up.

After Jesse left, he slumped on the narrow bed and looked at the small room with spartan furniture. While the house wasn't too big, it was big enough to house four rooms and a lounge. Apparently, the farm was sold at a reasonable price, and the money that his father was making wasn't bad, and things seemed steady. Jeff was glad that was the case. He laid down on the bed and soon drifted into sleep.

The whole family congregated at the dinner table that night, even his drunken father. Joey was excited to see him and had too many questions for him. Whereas his father simply nodded at him to acknowledge his presence. Fortunately, Jeff was too detached to care, and his mother's cooking made him forget the rest of his woes. It had been forever since he had a home-cooked meal. The roast with gravy and biscuits was delicious.

Afterward, his brother told him that his father was still drinking all the time and had refused to sell the farm to their Uncle when he decided to place the farm on the market.

"Uncle Roger doesn't visit that often no more, not after the ugly fight he and Dad had after the farm. Plus, moving to the city also put distance between us," Joey told him.

"I suppose he doesn't know I'm in town," Jeff mused.

"Yeah ... suppose you should go see him."

"Yeah, I will," Jeff nodded.

"Jeffy, you've become a fine man." His Uncle embraced him with pride. His weather-beaten face was red from exertion, as well as emotions at seeing his beloved nephew.

"And you've become an old man," Jeff teased.

He'd decided to visit his Uncle first thing in the morning, and getting out of the city toward the familiar road leading to his farm had made him both nostalgic and excited. He looked forward to meeting his Uncle more than his own father because his Uncle was the one who had truly raised him and made him the man he was.

"Now tell me all about your adventures in Vietnam. I wanna know everything," his Uncle said.

"I'd like to visit Gramps' grave first if it's alright with you. I wanna pay my respects." Jeff looked away, a sheen in his eyes.

"Sure," his Uncle nodded in understanding.

The two men silently drove toward the cemetery, and once Jeff was at his Grandfather's grave, his Uncle left him alone and walked away, giving him privacy. Jeff appreciated it; he lowered the flowers on the stone and reverently read the tombstone.

"Look, Gramps, I made it back in one piece. I hope I made you proud," Jeff said, blinking back his tears.

Later, both the Uncle and nephew reminisced about the old times, and Jeff told him about the atrocities he saw in Vietnam and the near-death experience he had over there.

"With the enemy closing in, I thought I was gone, but I would rather die at my own hands than let those barbarians get to me. I was this close to shooting myself when I was rescued," Jeff told his Uncle.

"Boy, am I glad to see you in one piece. This is what your Gramps feared till his last breath, that his golden boy wouldn't survive," Roger told him.

Jeff nodded, lost for words. "Have you spoken to Pa after that fight?"

"Nope, we've crossed paths in town. I've heard he's making a decent living, but honestly, I don't have a lot to say to him," his Uncle shrugged.

"Hmmm, he's still the same, though, a drunkard and a wife-beater," Jeff grimaced.

"A leopard doesn't change its spots, Jeff. Your father can never change," Roger told him.

"If you touch her again, I'm gonna blow your head off!" Jeff screamed at his father.

He'd seen his father knocking his mother around a couple of times, but every time he caught him raising his hand on her or getting ready to beat her, Jeff had intervened, telling his father to take a hike. The two had once again locked horns on this matter, often verbally abusing each other. But today, his father had come home drunk and struck her on the cheek. Seeing this, Jeff lost it.

"Don't ya dare tell me how ta treat ma own woman . . . " his father's words slurred, and he swayed on his feet.

"You're pathetic." Jeff looked at him in disgust and took his mother out of the room, furious with her as well for putting up with this treatment.

"Why don't you stop him? Why tolerate this abuse? Just kick him down the curb!" he spoke angrily.

"I'm used to it. Besides, where will he go? He'll come back begging, and I'll have to take him in. Too much hassle. So, don't worry about us," she shrugged.

However, not long after this incident, his mother's words came to bite her as his father started drinking more heavily, and his behavior became more erratic. He went after her one-to-many times, one day crossing all limits and almost belting her when she got too furious and pushed him back with force. She took out the gun and shot him in the shoulder. His father was too stunned to even howl in pain in the initial few minutes. Hell, the whole family was too stunned at such a bold step; they all later laughed about it, saying he had it coming. He had pushed her a little too many times, and this was her revenge. After that, Jeff's father sobered up enough to realize that he could no longer use his wife as a punching bag.

One thing that Jeff splurged on after being back was buying a Harley and shooting the breeze. He visited all his old haunts and even started a summer romance with his high school sweetheart, just having fun and nothing serious.

So, for the next couple of months, he just hung around town, frequented all the bars, regaled people with his war stories, and, of course, fooled around with his fling. But once again, the course of his life was about to change.

One day, he got an invite to go to Washington, D.C.. He had been invited to the White House to meet President Nixon. The President wanted to give him a medal of honor as promised by the Sergeant back in Da Nang. Jeff had forgotten about it all, but now that it was happening, he felt anticipation.

When Jeff arrived at the White House, he was in awe of its grandeur, but more than that, he couldn't believe he was about to meet the U.S. President. Walking toward the Oval Office, he took everything in; the entire place felt something out of a movie set, not that he had been to one, but still.

Walking into the Oval Office, he saw the 37th President of the United States of America seated behind a large desk, surrounded by armed guards and officials. Jeff was asked to step forward, and introductions were made. President Nixon had a stocky build and intelligent dark eyes. He thanked Jeff for his services to the country and told him that he would be awarded a medal for his valor.

"Well, thank you, sir. But is there any way I can swap the medal with cash as a reward for my services? You see, money is more helpful for a war veteran looking for their next job than a medal. Doesn't pay bills, you see," Jeff replied, sounding straightforward.

The President and his people were taken aback by such bluntness, but then he laughed.

"You're an interesting man. I see … so how much money are we talking about here?"

"Well, 50,000 dollars would be a sweet deal," Jeff told him boldly.

"I see; let me confer with my people and see if you can be rewarded that instead," the President told him. Jeff nodded and was led outside to wait. He waited for a while but was soon asked back inside.

"So, tell me this, soldier, what can we do about people that are in the way or want to harm the U.S. and make sure nothing goes wrong—on the border of the law?" he asked Jeff, point blank.

Jeff gave it some thought and then replied, "You can't tell the police to kill someone or even military personnel, but you can sure tell a civilian to do so and later can give them a pardon for it."

"Interesting, that is a very good reasoning." The President steepled his fingers together.

"Sorry to jump the gun, sir, but are you saying what I think you're saying?" Jeff asked.

"And what do you think I'm saying, soldier?" he inquired.

"That you want some people eliminated," Jeff answered.

The President gave Jeff a long look and then got out of his seat and stepped toward him. "Exactly, and I think you're just the man for the job. You're going to lead my team. I'm calling you First Elite One!" he shook Jeff's hands and smiled at him.

Jeff looked around the room, where only a few people who were closer to the man in charge stood with passive expressions, their body language guarded. There was an energy shift in the room as if a monumental moment in the history of the U.S. was unfolding. And it was true, for this was the beginning of what would much later be known to the world as Homeland Security.

The Origins

Although Homeland Security was officially founded after the 9/11 attacks in 2001 and was decreed by President Bush, the Secret Service working in anonymity in the U.S. started at the end of the 19th century. Making it America's oldest federal law enforcement agency, it was initially created in 1865 to stamp out rampant counterfeiting in order to stabilize America's newly budding financial system. By the end of the Civil War, nearly one-third of all currency in circulation was forged. It was a major issue for the authorities, and it was affecting the country's financial stability, bringing it into jeopardy. To counter this, the Secret Service was established in 1865 as a bureau in the Treasury Department to suppress widespread counterfeiting.

Apart from countering counterfeit money, another major reason for the need to establish a Secret Service was because of the assassination of President McKinley in 1901. The Secret Service was tasked with the full-time protection of the President of the United States after that. Although, as history would witness, it failed to do so in certain situations, but at that time, this was the primary reason. Over time, this protective mission has been expanded by statutory changes, Presidential Decision Directives, Homeland Security Presidential Directives, National Security Presidential Directives, and various Executive Orders.

Currently, the Secret Service is mandated by Congress with two distinct and critical national security missions: protecting the nation's leaders and safeguarding the financial and critical infrastructure of the United States. It is also tasked with protecting the White House Complex and Naval Observatory. Since 1970, the Uniformed Division has also been responsible for protecting foreign embassies and consulates in and around the Washington, D.C., area.

However, all this was to come much later. When President Nixon decided to establish a Secret Service Division named Elite One, it was primarily to deal with State and Non-State Actors who were a threat to the United States.

The silence in the room was unnerving, especially the way the President was looking at Jeff expectantly. Jeff knew that from this day forward, whatever decision he was about to make was going to be monumental as well as life-changing.

All things considered, he knew entangling yourself in White House business was like getting caught in a spider's web, yet having traversed through the war zone that Vietnam was and having escaped with his life intact, Jeff knew he could do it. Besides, the money was a sweet deal, and he needed it, so without any preamble, Jeff replied to President Nixon's query, "I'm your man, Sir."

President Nixon nodded with a slight smile on his face, ordered a briefcase with $50,000 in it, and handed it to Jeff. He motioned Jeff to sit opposite him, and Jeff, who had been rocking on his feet for a while now, was relieved to be seated.

"Your team will deal with me directly under the Secret Service. You will get your information on a 3 • 5 note card until we figure out something else," President Nixon explained.

Then he beckoned one of his aides to debrief about how the whole operation would start as well as the technicalities related to it. They talked about anything and everything that could or would happen in the country and around the world.

"Basically, you come in when the others are limited or stopped. Your job is to clean up the mess and also get those tasks done that are classified and can't be traced. You, Jeff, are the final trick up our sleeves," President Nixon told him.

Jeff nodded, understanding that his operations were going to be clandestine, and he agreed. That day in the White House, all the people present in that room had an understanding that if Jeff were given an order, he would carry it out and assemble a team that could be so diverse at tracking people, situations, threats, and acts by anyone to anything you could imagine.

"Your team has to be filled with people who have diverse skills and can work undercover as well as under pressure. They can't be queasy about getting their hands dirty or bloodied," the aide said.

"As well as people who are discreet and understand what's at stake because it's imperative that you have people who know how to fly under the radar and know how to blend in the background. Plus, the eminence of keeping their mouths shut no matter what. When building a Secret task force, the most important skill that needs to be instilled among the recruits is to learn never to share anything about their job with anyone . . ." another aide chimed in.

"I hope you're understanding what is being communicated to you," the President looked at Jeff pointedly.

"I understand and appreciate the opportunity," Jeff said solemnly.

He knew amassing and assembling the team would be his pride and joy. The kind of man that would protect the U.S. no matter what—men who had to be worthy enough to be part of the Elite team. Jeff stood up and shook hands with President Nixon. On his way out, the aide told him that soon someone would get in touch with him with his first assignment and that Jeff should know not to mention what transpired in that room with any outsider.

Jeff assured him he wouldn't be betraying confidences and would get on with starting to look for the right people to recruit for the team.

It was still surreal to have met the President, but more importantly, the money he had received was pretty amazing. It had been a week since the meeting, and he had been wondering when he would get his first assignment. By then, he had rented a small one room apartment in town and moved out of his home.

He was sitting at his desk, engrossed in his thoughts, when the shrill ring of his phone shattered the silence. Startled, he reached for the receiver and brought it to his ear.

"Hello?" he answered, his voice filled with curiosity.

"Is this Jeff?" a deep voice asked on the other end.

"Yes, speaking," Jeff replied, his heart pounding in his chest.

"This is Agent Johnson. We have a matter of utmost importance to discuss with you," the voice continued.

Jeff's mind raced, his thoughts jumping to various possibilities. He had been waiting for a call, but now that the gears were turning in motion, Jeff felt a little unnerved.

"Check your mailbox; you've been left with the coordinates for the location you have to be at, along with the time. Be punctual. I hate waiting," Agent Johnson warned.

"But wait, how did you . . . " before he could finish his sentence, the call had been cut.

"How did they find out where I'm renting? I'm not even using my real name," Jeff mused as he stood up and hurried downstairs to check the mailbox. There in the mailbox was a 3 x 5 card with information for the meetup.

"We have received intelligence that a man, known only as Mr. X, has made a credible threat to assassinate President Nixon," Agent Johnson explained, his voice steady and serious.

Jeff's breath caught in his throat as he absorbed the weight of the situation. He knew that as an elite force agent, his duty was to protect the President at all costs. However, the thought of taking a life was a heavy burden to bear. The location of their meeting had been a lone dilapidated warehouse just on the outskirts of Nashville, and Jeff had to leave for the place in the middle of the night to make it on time.

"Your first assignment is to neutralize the threat posed by Mr. X. We have reason to believe he will attempt to carry out his plan within the next few days," Agent Johnson continued.

Jeff's mind was in turmoil, torn between duty and morality. He knew that the President's life was in imminent danger, and it was his duty to safeguard him. But the thought of taking someone's life, regardless of their intentions, went against his core values.

"I understand the gravity of the situation, Agent Johnson," Jeff replied, his voice faltering slightly. "But is there no other way? Can we not apprehend him and bring him to justice?"

Agent Johnson sighed audibly; his voice tinged with sympathy. "We have explored all available options, but the urgency of the threat leaves us with no alternative. Our intelligence suggests that Mr. X is highly trained and determined. The only way to ensure the President's safety is to eliminate the threat completely. And you knew your hands would get dirty when you took on the job. I sure as hell hope you're not reneging on the deal," the Agent said.

Jeff closed his eyes, trying to steady his racing thoughts. He pictured President Nixon and the conversation they had in that secret room; he thought of the countless lives that could be affected by the outcome of this mission. After a long pause, he finally found his voice.

"Agent Johnson. I made a deal, and don't back down from my word. I understand the gravity of this mission; I will do what needs to be done to protect the President," Jeff said, his voice filled with determination.

Agent Johnson nodded, and the two men shook hands. He passed Jeff a slim dossier that contained every detail, as well as what needed to be done in order to eliminate the threat.

Jeff prepared himself mentally and physically for the task ahead. He knew that the next few days would test his limits, but he was committed to fulfilling his duty and finishing the job that he had been tasked with.

So, now with a game plan set in his mind, he started assembling a team of experts in every field, from snipers to geeks, that could find out anything and destroy it within a matter of days. He started recruiting veterans he had worked with in Vietnam who could be trusted. He also started bringing all types of people on board: snipers, computer gurus, hackers, trackers, bounty hunters, and anyone who could fill positions similar to Homeland Security of today's time.

The man who tried to kill President Nixon was shot in his car at long range, about 400 yards, and Jeff lay and waited for him for days to come down that particular road.

Jeff set everything up in about a year, as it took time to find the people he needed. It was easy to find someone to kill someone as a lot of the guys coming back from Vietnam were begging to kill someone. It was twisted, but this is what war does to you. It chips away your humanity and makes most of the war veterans a killing machine, and once that's been hard-wired into the psyche, it becomes difficult to go back from it. Therefore, finding killers was not difficult; controlling them and honing their skills to complete their jobs and not get carried away was what he needed to do.

Now the task force that he wanted to assemble was pretty much in place. The Elite One Secret Service Wing was a properly functioning faction. If one were to ask what Elite One was? Then, in simple words, it was a man who was put in charge of taking care of anything and everything that the U.S. government wanted or needed, especially clandestine tasks that couldn't be documented.

Elite One headquarters was in Nashville, Tennessee, and it was based there because Jeff wanted access to the capital of Tennessee basement, where they met and operated out of. Elite One was an independent unit of the CIA and FBI and only dealt with the Secret Service.

When the WUO—Weather Underground Organization (U.S. terrorist group, aka Weathermen) released the book *Prairie Fire* to indicate the need for a unified Communist Party, Elite One started busting in on them and taking them out one or two at a time. Between 1976-1981, the Weather Underground began to disband, and many members were turning themselves in. With the federal government dropping most charges in 1973 and President Carter's amnesty for draft dodgers, they disbanded completely. During this time, Jeff had to kill about 5 people for the government, and his team was responsible for about 15 total deaths. They had illegal wiretaps and intelligence sources and methods issued that they had a good handle on to keep abreast of what was going on everywhere.

It was their job to survey, observe, and report any internal or external threat to the National Security of the US as well as a personal threat to the President himself.

Over the course of time, they got assignments to rescue five DEA agents out of Mexico, and Jeff flew in with a DC3 with an M16 and M148 grenade launcher. His team blew the side of the jail out and the agents started running for the plane. A Jeep with a 50-caliber machine guns on it came at the plane. Jeff had the engines running and hung out the window and blew up the Jeep with three Mexicans in it.

The missions were an adrenaline rush for Jeff, and he was really coming into his element, but most importantly, he was proud of the team he had amassed and was looking forward to what was to come.

Elite One

Jeff stood tall and composed, his gaze focused and unwavering. Dressed in a sharp black suit and a discreet earpiece, he exuded an air of confidence and authority. But behind his calm demeanor, he was sweating under the collar.

His unit had been running covert operations for the presidency ever since Elite One had been formed. Every time a mission was assigned to them, it was a given that Jeff and his men would be putting their lives on the line because they were always called in when things were going sideways or someone needed to get a messy job done that couldn't be traced back to the government.

His journey into the clandestine world of government service began with rigorous training and an unyielding commitment to assembling a unit that would become known for its skills. Luckily, from the early stages, his exceptional skills in surveillance, combat, and strategic thinking helped him both in Mexico as well as when he took out the man who threatened to kill President Nixon. He had also rounded up some of the most cut-throat men to be within the elite ranks of the agency.

So, today shouldn't have been this daunting. However, Jeff knew that while the task itself wasn't something new and they had been shipping people covertly in and out of the U.S. since their conception, the stakes were high, and flying an infamous military leader of a country was a highly sensitive job.

"Is the team Alpha in position?" he asked in a small walkie-talkie in his hand.

"Affirmative," the man responded to Jeff, listening via his earpiece.

Jeff then asked about the position of team Beta, and after confirming the coordinates, he started pacing the room because, as of now, it was a waiting game. The dice were about to be rolled. He looked outside the big window into the dark night and thought about all the years that had taken him to build this life, but more than that, how his life had changed completely after the meeting at the White House.

Elite One's missions often took Jeff and his team to the farthest corners of the world, where danger lurked in the shadows. One such operation led him to the sun-soaked streets of Guatemala, a country plagued by corruption and violence. Guatemala was a hotbed for all kinds of criminal activity as the police-to-citizen ratio was completely off balance, and a lot of bribery went into circumventing the anti-drug police and other police departments to get their way. Arms and drug trafficking were rampant, and the biggest reason for violence in Latin America was, and still is, due to the illicit arms trade.

The U.S. government sought his expertise in combating the escalating arms trade that fueled the chaos. With his specialized knowledge, Jeff organized covert operations to intercept illicit firearms shipments, disrupting the operations of criminal organizations. From there on out, he ran guns for the government to Guatemala and brought drugs back for government testing.

Later, a new chapter began in Jeff's life when he was assigned a different role within the agency. This time, he found himself at the helm of an airplane, serving as a pilot for Eastern Airlines. This seemingly innocuous position granted him an opportunity to expand his horizons further. Under the guise of a legitimate airline operation, Jeff started using his position to transport confiscated drugs back to the United States for disposal and run his clandestine operation of bringing in a couple of kilos of cocaine through Miami.

The thrill of his double life escalated when a mysterious man approached Jeff, offering him a substantial sum to transport cargo to Jamaica and the Bahamas. That man had offered Jeff 100 grand to fly to Jamaica and the Bahamas, and he did it for the money.

Driven by financial gain and the opportunity to do something new, he was excited. Little did he know that this decision would change his life forever. From that point on, he started hauling it for himself and making half a million dollars a trip.

Jeff ran about 26 of these trips and had so much cash he did not know what to do with it.

Of course, ever since he had started making extra money, he helped out his family as much as he could and even gave money to his Uncle, too. But still, it was too much cash.

Jeff was spending it living high on the hog. To protect his operation, Jeff employed a clever ploy. He bought two airplanes with the same N number on both of them with identical transponders, so they looked exactly alike. In the United States, the registration number is commonly referred to as an N number, as all aircraft registered in the U.S. have a number starting with the letter N.

He left one aircraft at the Lewisburg airport with a flat tire and flew the other one on the trips. He would fly the other plane on his smuggling trips, blending in seamlessly with legitimate air traffic.

Upon arrival at his destinations, Jeff expertly offloaded the contraband to trusted local contacts, including the sheriff, who acted as a reliable intermediary for the safe transportation of the drugs. Over time, Jeff meticulously paid off key individuals, from customs agents to air traffic controllers, ensuring his smooth passage through the treacherous world he navigated.

Running drugs and other contraband items on commercial planes, or any other aircraft for that matter, was a very risky business, and one needs to have a backup plan as well as enough contacts to sail through aviation checks and customs to smuggle without getting caught. So, it was imperative to not only know the right people who have the authority to get you through the red tape but also to have enough cash to oil their hands.

If there was one thing Jeff had learned in all these years was networking and how to make contacts. While expanding his team, he had consistently expanded his network and made friends in all the right places. Hence, for him to run his drug smuggling operation smoothly was not that big of an issue; he had full confidence in pulling it off. Soon enough, this became a way of life for him, and from 1978 to 1986, he ran a steady and monthly charter to Cartagena, South America, to refuel in the Bahamas. He ran from Boscobel, Jamaica, to the Bahamas, not only to refuel but also to drop the pot to cigarette boats that would pick it all up and take it in to keep everyone involved in the smuggling business from being detected. Jeff was always free to run when and how he and the others involved wanted.

From there, he would be coming in as a low approach to the Miami or Fort Lauderdale airport to pick up a flight plan and fly directly to Tennessee, always landing at night when no one could see anything.

With each successful trip, Jeff's notoriety grew. His flights became known as the stuff of legends, shrouded in secrecy and whispered among those who dared to dabble in the underworld. The sheer amount of money he accumulated seemed surreal, and he struggled to find ways to hide his wealth.

"All that running around has made you soft; you need to practice harder," the Grandmaster scolded Jeff as he pinned him down on the mat.

"I do work harder, but you always have a sneak move up your sleeve," Jeff grunted as the Grandmaster exerted more pressure on him, making Jeff gasp.

"Fine, I'll be more consistent with training," Jeff choked, and the Grandmaster relented and helped him get up.

"I'm going in the back room; let me know if anyone needs me," the Grandmaster called out as he criticized the form of a few other people while on his way to the backroom.

Jeff was working out in the Karate studio, sweating profusely, when he felt the people in the studio going quiet, and a hush fell over him. He swiveled around to see what was happening and had to do a double take when he saw the famous singer Elvis Presley walk into the studio.

His eyes fell on Jeff, and he made a beeline for him.

"Hi, I'm Elvis. Perhaps you know me?" he gave Jeff a disarming smile.

"Well, of course."

"Anyway, I've heard that this studio has some of the best fighters in the area, and I am looking for another bodyguard. So, I want to know who is the best one here? And if he wants a real job and is willing to come to work for me?" Elvis asked, looking around.

"Well, outside of the Grandmaster, I am the best," Jeff told him.

"Interesting, and how do you know that?"

"I don't need to know it. I know for a fact."

"Well, if you can beat my main man, I will give you the job," he told Jeff.

Jeff felt a thrill of excitement course through him. He liked the adrenaline rush it gave him, and he felt excited to prove himself.

"Sure, let's get on with it. Bring your best," Jeff agreed.

Needless to say, it took about a minute to knock Elvis's bodyguard out cold. The man was huge and a good fighter, but he was no match for Jeff, who was the best of the best. His years of Taekwondo and Karate practice had made him lethal and a killing machine, and he aimed to become a Grandmaster soon, so it was no wonder that for Jeff to take on the big man was no challenge. Besides, in Karate, stealth mattered, not size.

Elvis clapped as he came forward and shook Jeff's hand.

"You're hired," Elvis told him.

Jeff was now working part-time for Eastern Airlines and then working part-time for Elvis. In the course of his stint as a bodyguard for the singer, Jeff came to realize that Elvis was attacked by women like no other person in history.

Jeff had to break women's fingers and twist their arms as they tried to tear the clothes off of him. He was flying Monday to Wednesday and then doing bodyguard work Friday to Sunday.

Life was fast-paced, and both jobs demanded his full attention. He was still working for the government when they called to keep his Elite One position, in which they were now up to 20 men, all working on the security of the United States and performing tasks that were demanded of them.

"Team Alpha, reporting . . . subject has left for the destination, we are tracking," the walkie-talkie cackled, and Jeff's remanence of the past was broken. Alert, he quickly responded.

"Team Beta, take your positions. The subject should not be let out of our sight...keep me posted. I'm heading to ground zero."

Ending communication, he quickly looked at his watch and surveyed the room, ensuring he left nothing important behind him. He walked along the long hotel corridor and knocked on the Presidential suite, where two bodyguards were already manning the door.

"What took you so long? We've been waiting." A thin man opened the door and scowled at him.

"Apologies, my teams are in place. The subject has left the special aircraft and is on his way to Ground Zero. I'm heading there; we will retrieve him," Jeff explained, scanning the room and looking at the figure of authority sitting in the middle of the room on a high-backed chair.

"Make sure you do that; your entire team is on the line," the U.S. Chief Marshal ordered.

Jeff nodded, understanding the threat, then left the room. He took the lift to the basement and headed for his car. Getting in, he thought about the man in question and how desperate the U.S. government was to bring him in. He also knew that failure at this job would not be forgiven and the consequences would be disastrous. He wished he would have taken an early retirement and focused on his side hustles. But he was a man wanting power, money, and thrill, so here he was once again, running a high-risk operation and putting everything on the line.

Jeff had to be a sniper and shoot about four different people, mostly in the U.S., who were in the way of the government. Although his team had become adept at getting things done and his side businesses kept him busy, he only stepped in when needed. While working for all three places, each of them knew about the other jobs, so they had a clear understanding of Jeff's role with the government. If and when the government called, they received priority.

Eastern had backup pilots, and Elvis had another bodyguard to fill in. So, when the orders came in, Jeff was off to assist or lead his Elite force to the next task.

When the government demanded that he bring their target to the U.S. and hide him, he was explicitly told to make sure everything ran smoothly. Manuel Antonio Noriega, former Military Leader of Panama, was the man to be brought back from Panama and then put on trial here in the U.S..

Jeff's task had been to oversee the transport from the private airbase to the hotel where he was to be hidden and watched for two days.

Noriega was subsequently convicted on eight counts of drug trafficking, racketeering, and money laundering and was sentenced to 40 years in prison. His sentence was later reduced to 30 years.

After ten days of constantly fighting and hiding in Panama, Noriega surrendered on January 3, 1990. He was detained as a prisoner of war, and later, another Elite One team, along with the CIA, took him to the United States.

Jeff wondered why it was imperative to make the man stand trial as he was a high-risk prisoner. They didn't want him killed and just wanted him out of the way and in prison. There had been other military personnel who had been taken out of the way as they were not killed. They were flown to

China and put in condos the U.S. had built for those who needed to be out of the way and not terminated. Having flown people to China and seeing how they were treated so well, Jeff had wondered about the whole scenario, and truth be told, he wouldn't have minded a condo himself over there.

A rueful smile came on his lips as he thought about it. He reached Ground Zero, the private airbase, and scanned the area, knowing his team was already in place to counter anything or any situation that might arise.

He waited for clearance from the higher-ups, and when a large black SUV stopped only a few feet away from Jeff's own car, he signaled his team, and men from Team Alpha jogged toward the SUV and transported Noriega to another vehicle.

The main airbase where Noriega's plane had landed and then the transport to this small private airstrip had been done without a hitch. Now, it was time to take him to the hotel and babysit him until his capture was announced officially.

Federal Prisoner No. 41586

“Received Noriega from Ground Zero, transporting him to the destination now.” Jeff radioed as soon as Noriega sat in the car. “Over.”

“So, drug trafficking, huh?” Jeff said as he lit a cigarette and put it in his mouth.

Noriega didn’t reply; instead, he stared at Jeff for a second and turned his head in the opposite direction, thinking about the day he surrendered.

It was Christmas Eve when he faced a U.S. indictment for narco-trafficking and electoral fraud. General "Mad Max" Thurman ordered the construction of a musical barrier to smoke him out. A constant barrage of sound played from the speakers that encircled the embassy.

As he was still hiding inside the embassy, the first day was something of a truce; it was Christmas music. But after that, things rapidly descended toward classic rock. "I am an opera fan." He would whisper inside as they blasted "Welcome to the Jungle" by Guns N' Roses, "God Bless the USA" by Lee Greenwood, and several other songs by Twisted Sister, The Doors, Black Sabbath, and most worryingly of all, "If I Had a Rocket Launcher" by Bruce Cockburn. This music frenzy and the dangerous dance that was going on between him and the authorities was now too exhausting. Noriega could no longer resist it, so he surrendered.

While Noriega was still lost in his thoughts, a sudden commotion burst the bubble of his nostalgia.

Suddenly, a group of armed men emerged on bikes, their faces masked and rifles aimed at the vehicle Noriega was in with Jeff.

"Ambush! Hold on tight!" Jeff shouted as he swerved the car to avoid the oncoming attack.

Bullets peppered the car, shattering windows and puncturing tires. Jeff expertly maneuvered, evading the onslaught as best as he could. The bodyguards returned fire, but the assailants seemed relentless, determined to take down the diplomatic convoy. In the chaos, Jeff radioed for backup, "I need backup! We're under attack. Someone has leaked information. I repeat, I NEED BACKUP!"

The attackers seemed well-prepared, setting up roadblocks and laying traps to slow them down. But Jeff was quick-witted and found alternative routes to keep them moving, navigating the roads at high speed. With backup finally closing in, Jeff saw an opportunity to outmaneuver their attackers. He took a sharp turn onto a narrow dirt path, leading the assailants away from the main road. The sudden change of direction left the attackers momentarily disoriented, and Jeff pushed the car to its limits, speeding through rough terrain and bouncing over rocks and potholes.

As they approached a steep hill, Jeff noticed a small riverbed below. Without hesitation, he accelerated toward the edge of the hill, soaring through the air before landing with a bone-jarring thud on the other side of the riverbank. The attackers, unable to follow such a risky path, were forced to give up the chase.

Breathing heavily, Jeff glanced at Noriega. "Are you alright?" he asked, genuinely concerned for his well-being.

"Yes, I am fine," Noriega replied, his voice steady despite the harrowing ordeal.

Their journey was far from over, but the worst immediate danger had passed. They regrouped with the backup team and continued their journey toward the city, where they would keep Noriega in a safe place until his court trial. However, Jeff remained vigilant, cautious that the attackers might attempt another assault.

Jeff led Noriega to a secure and undisclosed location, a maximum-security prison cell in Miami. "This will be your new home for a while," Jeff said as he unlocked the main door to the cell.

In the following days, Jeff maintained a watchful eye on the incarcerated former leader. Noriega's arrogance had been replaced by humility as he no longer saw himself as untouchable, and the stark reality of his situation weighed heavily on his soul.

As Jeff sat in his room, his phone rang. "Hello?"

"Hello? Is this Jeff? The private bodyguard service provider?"

"Who's this?"

"I am Verse."

"Verse, who?"

"The rapper Verse, Verse Shakur. Don't you recognize me?"

"Oh yes, yes." Jeff paused. "What do you want, Mr. Shakur."

"Well, I called a private bodyguard. Haven't I?" Verse sighed. "I've heard you're the best in the business, and I need your help, man."

"Sir, I am no private bodyguard services provider; I just do it for Elvis."

"Look, man, my life is in danger, and I need someone I can trust to be my bodyguard. I've been involved in some stuff I shouldn't have, and now people are after me."

"I understand, but you need to be upfront with me. Are you involved in drug dealing?"

"Yeah, man, I got mixed up in it a while back. But I'm trying to get out of that life now."

"Look, I can't do it. I have some other important business to do."

"I get it, man, but I'm willing to pay you double whatever you're getting paid now. I need the best protection out there."

"Listen, I can't help you. I'm already committed to another important government mission right now, and I can't leave that behind. I'm sorry, but I won't be able to take on your request." And with that, Jeff put back the receiver.

Verse was an East Coast rap music artist. Rap culture was all about rocking chains, venting your money, flexing gang affiliations, and being hard to the core. Rappers required fat investments from the jump: the more money they put in, the higher the return. So, the number of expensive materials directly determined the credibility of a rapper, which translated to more media attention, radio play, and so forth. With that being said, some rappers worked 9 to 5 jobs, while others got impatient, like Verse, and got into drug dealing.

"As if I have nothing better to do than babysit rappers." Jeff scoffed as he put down the receiver.

The courtroom's atmosphere was tense as the ousted head of state, Manuel Antonio Noriega, stood before U.S. District Judge William Hoeveler. Noriega was clad in his military uniform, displaying the poise he was known for during his reign.

The room was filled with anticipation as the prosecution laid out the extensive list of allegations against Noriega. Among them was the accusation of conspiring with Colombia's notorious Medellin cartel to smuggle cocaine through Panama and into the streets of the United States.

As the charges were read aloud, Noriega stood resolute, refusing to acknowledge the court's authority or to enter a plea. His silence was palpable, an act of protest against the proceedings and a show of defiance against the system that sought to hold him accountable.

"Mr. Noriega, you are before this court to face the charges brought against you," Judge Hoeveler stated firmly. "Your refusal to acknowledge the court's authority will not hinder these proceedings. The accusations are grave."

Noriega remained silent, his face a mask of defiance. The court proceedings continued, with the prosecution presenting evidence of Noriega's involvement in drug trafficking and money laundering. Witnesses testified to the vast sums of money exchanged and the ruthless tactics employed to protect his illicit activities.

Jeff watched as the formal charges were read out. Noriega was accused of being a narcotics racketeer, orchestrating the flow of drugs and perpetuating the violence that had plagued countless lives. As the proceedings unfolded, Noriega's facade of invincibility crumbled. He was no longer the indomitable force he once believed himself to be but a man facing the consequences of his crimes.

The trial was a long and arduous process, with both sides presenting their arguments and evidence. The evidence against Noriega was overwhelming, and the jury didn't take long to reach a unanimous decision. Guilty on all counts. The once mighty leader was now a convicted felon, and the weight of his deeds settled upon him like an anchor. His legacy was forever tarnished.

After the verdict was pronounced, Jeff escorted Noriega out of the courtroom. Noriega's head hung low, and his steps were slow and deliberate as if coming to terms with the reality of his new life as a prisoner.

Jeff's job was done now; he had to wait for the next orders from the White House. Until then, he could do his part-time jobs.

Within the labyrinthine corridors of a maximum security facility, the nation's most prominent prisoner of the war on drugs now resided. Once an imposing figure who had styled himself as Panama's "Maximum Leader," he was now a mere federal prisoner, known only by 'Federal Prisoner No. 41586."

Behind the heavy steel doors of his cell, the man who had wielded power with an iron fist now confronted the harsh reality of his choices. And though he would later be extradited back to his country, for now, the U.S. judicial system prevailed.

Jeff groggily answered his ringing phone. He recognized the number; it was that rapper. "Hello, Jeff? Jeff, please, I need you to escort me to a safe house. Please make arrangements for me. I am ready to pay triple, not even double." His tone was serious this time; he was scared to death.

"Alright, fine. But first, you have to meet me. I must be sure and know everything about what type of threat you're facing."

"Oh, thank you. Thank you so much; you have no idea about the burden you have lifted from my shoulders."

They met at a coffee shop; Verse was hiding his face in a black hoodie, trying to escape the threat.

"Hey man, thanks for meeting me." Verse said as he looked around the café, trying to stay away from the threat that might be lurking around him.

"You don't have to do that in my presence, Verse," Jeff noticed his fear.

"Do what?"

"Fearing for your life." Jeff raised his eyebrows, emphasizing that they were safe there as he had already double-checked the place.

"So, would you escort me to the safe house?"

"Yes! But only if you're still willing to pay me the promised money."

"I will. I will. I even brought advance with me." Verse took out a black briefcase from under the table and slid it toward Jeff.

"Hmm." Jeff nodded as he took the briefcase under his possession. "I'll text you the time and venue for tomorrow. You'll have to meet me there, and I will escort you to a safe house. But to be safe, we have to take Mexico's route. So, our first destination is Mexico, and then Guatemala, your safehouse will be there. Consider this as your vacation."

"Alright, Jeff. Let's meet tomorrow." With that, they shook hands, and both parted their ways in opposite directions.

The next day, Jeff received a call again from Verse.

"Hello, Jeff? Jeff, please, we need to make a move now," Verse pleaded, his words rushing out anxiously. "Please, make arrangements for me."

"Whoa, slow down, Verse. What's going on? Are you in danger?" Concern replaced Jeff's sleepiness with a sharp focus.

Jeff's mind raced as he tried to figure out what to do. Jeff knew he couldn't just leave this much money hanging.

"Okay, Verse. I'll help you." Jeff said firmly. "Where are you now? I'll come and get you."

"I'm at the old warehouse," Verse whispered, his voice barely audible. "Hurry, Jeff. Please hurry."

Jeff quickly got dressed. He knew the warehouse Verse mentioned was a rundown place known for shady dealings.

Arriving at the warehouse, Jeff found Verse huddled in a corner, looking like a terrified animal. "Come on, Verse, we have to get out of here," Jeff said, pulling him up.

"I didn't mean to get involved in this mess," Verse stammered, tears streaming down his face. "I just wanted to make some quick money, but it was a nightmare. They called me here at 8:30, but I arrived early, at 8:00. They weren't expecting me; they didn't know I was already here, so they discussed their plan to kill me. I never showed up, and after waiting for an hour, they eventually left."

Jeff put a reassuring hand on Verse's shoulder. "It's going to be alright. I have a place where you can stay tonight, but we must be careful. Those people might still be looking for you. We will leave for Mexico tomorrow."

They made their way to an apartment that belonged to one of Jeff's contacts. Jeff helped Verse settle in, assuring him he would take care of everything.

As the hours passed, Jeff worked tirelessly to figure out how to extricate Verse from this dangerous situation. He made calls, pulled some strings, and tried to negotiate a way out. The people who were after Verse were not ones to be trifled with, and it seemed like an impossible task.

Throughout the day, Verse stayed hidden in the apartment.

Late in the evening, Jeff received a call with a potential way out. But it came with a heavy price. "They want a significant amount of money, Verse," Jeff explained. "I know you said you're willing to pay, but this is a substantial sum."

"I don't care, man." Verse said. "Money doesn't matter if I don't leave this alive."

Verse pooled his resources and managed to gather the demanded amount. It was risky, but Jeff hoped they could reach the safe house.

The next day, they met the intermediary at a discreet location, exchanging the money for Verse's safety.

The two hurriedly sat in the car that took them to the private airstrip, where a charter plane was waiting for them. Verse's money had got them this plane that Jeff was to pilot. He had already filed a flight plan under Verse's fake ID.

They landed on another private airstrip on the outskirts of Mexico City. A car was already waiting for them. They settled into the backseat, keeping their eyes peeled for any suspicious activity.

"Where are we going?" Verse asked.

"The less you know, the better," Jeff answered.

Jeff kept glancing in the rear-view mirror throughout the journey, half-expecting to see goons tailing Verse. Verse sat nervously, his eyes questioning Jeff from time to time.

"We've got a good plan, and the safe house is well-hidden. Just stay calm, and we'll get through this. The goons aren't expecting this." Jeff whispered, barely audible to himself as he tried to reassure Verse and himself.

"I hope you're right, man. I can't die before dropping my next album!" Verse managed to faint a smile, trying to lighten the mood amidst the tension.

"You'll drop that album, don't worry," Jeff grinned.

After what seemed like an eternity, they reached a small village near the Mexican border. There, they met Carlos, Jeff's trustworthy local contact who would guide them through the journey ahead.

"Hola, amigos. Ready to begin?" Carlos welcomed them with a warm smile.

"Yes, Carlos. We must reach the safe house as quickly and discreetly as possible," Jeff's expressions were stern.

"I know all the hidden routes. Follow me, and keep close," Carlos replied.

Jeff and Verse followed Carlos through dense forests and hidden paths, avoiding major roads and checkpoints. At times, they had to hide in abandoned shacks or under the cover of night to elude potential pursuers.

"This ... this is crazy!" Verse breathed heavily.

"Almost there, Verse. Just a little longer," Jeff reassured.

Finally, after days of nerve-wracking travel, they arrived at the safe house in Guatemala. The relief washed over them like a tidal wave.

"I still don't understand why we didn't take a flight to Guatemala?" Verse had complained.

"Because the people you're running from have connections in the Guatemalan Aviation industry, and I didn't want to mess with that," Jeff told him.

"You made it, amigos. Here's your safe house." Carlos pointed at the safe house.

"Thank you, Carlos." Verse said as he happily ran toward the house. He was safe, for now.

As Verse ran toward the house, Jeff told Carlos about his plan to stay for a day or two as he had to be sure that Verse was safe there, and then he would be back on his way to Miami as his job was done here.

"Until we meet again, my friend," Carlos said as he smiled when he and Jeff said their goodbyes to each other, standing at the front of the safe house.

Job in Gulf Tiger

Jeff was going about his day, relaxing after a rigorous training session, when his phone rang. He glanced at the caller ID and saw an unfamiliar number with a Dubai area code. "Now, who is this?" He whispered. Curiosity piqued, and he answered the call with furrowed eyebrows.

"Hello, this is Jeff speaking," he said, his voice laced with curiosity.

"Good day, Jeff. My name is Farid Al-Mansoori. I am the manager of the Sheikh in Dubai, Sheikh Al-Rashid," came the smooth, confident voice on the other end.

"Hello, Mr. Mansoori. What can I do for you?" Jeff replied, intrigued by the unexpected call.

"Well, Jeff, we've heard quite a lot about your skills as a bodyguard and pilot," Farid began, his tone hinting at something big. "Our Sheikh needs someone with your expertise and reputation to join his personal team,"

"I'm honored to be considered. Can you tell me more about the job?"

"This position is highly esteemed, Jeff. As the Sheikh's bodyguard and pilot, you'll be responsible for his safety during his travels, both within Dubai and internationally. It's a demanding role, but it comes with generous compensation and benefits," Farid explained.

Jeff couldn't believe his luck. A job that combined both his skills and passion, and with a Sheikh, no less! "That sounds incredible."

"I'm glad to hear that, Jeff. Your reputation precedes you. It's exactly what the Sheikh is looking for in his personal protection team," Farid continued. "The role also involves flying the Sheikh's private jet, so your piloting expertise will come in handy,"

"When would I be needed in Dubai?"

"We'd like to extend an invitation for you to visit Dubai and meet the Sheikh in person. You'll have the opportunity to see the surroundings and discuss the specifics of the role," Farid said warmly. "We'll cover all travel expenses, of course."

"I'm in. When do you want me there?" Jeff replied.

"We can arrange your travel for next week if that works for you. Will that be alright?" Farid inquired.

"Next week is perfect. I'll make sure to be there," Jeff confirmed.

"Excellent, Jeff. We're looking forward to meeting you. Safe travels, and we'll be in touch with all the necessary details soon." Farid said, his voice brimming with satisfaction.

Jeff settled into his seat on the aircraft that would carry him to Dubai. The plane's engine roared to life, and soon, it was soaring through the clear blue skies. The flight was nothing short of luxurious. The cabin had comfortable leather seats and soft ambient lighting. The attentive cabin crew provided impeccable service, offering gourmet meals.

Stepping off the plane, Jeff was greeted by the Sheikh's manager, Farid. Farid extended a hand in greeting as they met, his grip firm and friendly.

"Welcome to Dubai, Jeff. I'm Farid Al-Mansoori, the Sheikh's manager. It's a pleasure to meet you finally,"

"Thank you, Mr. Al-Mansoori. The pleasure is mine. I'm honored to be here and to work with Sheikh Al-Rashid," Jeff shook Farid's hand.

Farid continued, "You must know some things before you meet him. Sheikh Rashid values security immensely, and I do not doubt that your expertise will be of great value to him. Please be on high alert every time as he doesn't like people who don't do their job properly," they walked toward the black SUV that was waiting for them.

"Oh no, you don't have to worry about that. I am sure you hired me after detailed research, and I was the best you could find." Jeff smirked. "Right?"

"Yes, you sure are," Farid chuckled.

As they settled into the vehicle, Farid further explained to him, "Your role as his bodyguard goes beyond just protection; you'll be a crucial part of his inner circle. The Sheikh has a busy schedule, and you'll work closely with his security team to ensure his safety during public engagements and private moments. And I do not doubt that you're up to the task. Sheikh Rashid's security is the highest priority, and your dedication must be clear. Once we arrive at the residence, you'll have the chance to meet the security team and familiarize yourself with the protocols."

14 km from Dubai Airport, they traveled to reach the Zabeel Palace. Jeff was in awe as he saw the palace from afar. It was one of the most secure places on Earth.

The imposing white facade of Zabeel Palace stood tall against the clear blue sky. The gates swung open, and Jeff stepped through as his vigilant gaze swept across the palace grounds.

The palace was surrounded by the vibrant flowers lining the pathways, their delicate fragrance carried by the gentle breeze, and the towering palm trees swayed gracefully. Jeff followed Farid as they walked along the cobblestone path that led to the palace's main entrance. The soft rustle of leaves accompanied their footsteps, creating a soothing backdrop to their conversation.

Farid, a dignified man in a tailored suit, shared insights into the history of Zabeel Palace as they approached. "This palace has been a residence of the royal family for generations. You see, Jeff, its architectural beauty is a blend of traditional design and modern luxury."

"Woah, it's a beauty!" Jeff's eyes gazed at the palace.

Nearing the entrance, the intricate details of the palace's facade became more apparent. Ornate carvings adorned the columns and archways, depicting scenes from historical events. The sun's rays shone on the marble surface.

The massive wooden doors creaked open, revealing the splendor that lay within. A grand foyer stretched before them, its marble floor polished to a mirror-like shine. A crystal chandelier hung from the ceiling.

Farid led Jeff through the foyer and into a vast courtyard that lay at the palace—a pool adorned with water lilies surrounded by tiles in shades of blue and green. In the distance, a gentle waterfall cascaded down a stone wall.

They took a right under the arcades, where a series of paintings were hung. Following the main road, they arrived at a room with a family tree of the ruling family as well as the portraits of the Sheikh. Then, they went outside in a courtyard with a pool and headed to the multi-story building. The Sheik was seated there as they went up to the first floor.

They ascended a grand marble staircase of the building. On the landing, ornate double doors beckoned them into a lavish reception room. Floor-to-ceiling windows framed breathtaking views of the city's skyline and the glistening Arabian Gulf beyond.

Finally, they entered a lavish chamber where the Sheikh awaited him. Dressed in regal attire, the Sheikh was seated on his chair.

Farid knocked on the door and introduced Jeff.

"I've been looking forward to meeting you. Welcome!" The Sheikh greeted.

Jeff offered a respectful nod and replied, "Thank you, Sheikh. The pleasure is all mine."

As they settled into the chairs, the Sheikh began. "I've heard exceptional things about your skills as a bodyguard and a pilot. My security team spoke highly of your expertise."

"I'm honored to have the opportunity to be of service," Jeff replied.

The Sheikh leaned forward; his keen gaze fixed on Jeff. "You see, I have unique requirements. I am in need of a bodyguard who can also serve as my personal pilot."

"I am up for the challenge, and I think you might know that recently, I transported a rapper to a safehouse UNDETECTED." Jeff paused. "I have undergone rigorous training and experience handling various situations, so you don't have to worry, Sheikh."

"Yes, yes, I know you come highly recommended both with personal security and moving contraband items within and out of states undetected. We know you have shown exceptional skills. At least that's what my security team told me," The Sheikh smiled as he shifted his gaze to Farid.

"I will ensure your safety and fulfill my duties to the best of my abilities," Jeff assured him.

A smile tugged at the corner of Sheikh's lips. "Very well, Jeff. We will provide you with all the necessary resources and ensure your comfortable stay here. You will learn and train for the next two days, and then you can officially start your job."

"Thank you," Jeff said as he stood up from his seat, and the manager showed him to his room.

"Jeff, the Sheikh's meeting in Abu-Dhabi was moved up. You'll be piloting the jet and accompanying him as his bodyguard. We need to depart immediately." Farid spoke through the earpiece.

"Understood, Mr. Al-Mansoori. The jet is prepped and ready to go. We'll be in the air in no time."

Jeff led them the way up the stairs to the aircraft. The Sheikh settled into a plush seat, and Jeff took his seat at the controls, his focus intensified. He went through the pre-flight checklist, ensuring every detail was in order. His hands moved across the instrument panel, his mind calculated the flight plan, and the jet taxied to the runway.

The runway stretched ahead, illuminated by the runway lights. Jeff's grip tightened on the controls as he smoothly guided the jet on the runway, building up speed. With a final surge of power, the aircraft lifted off the ground, ascending into the sky.

Jeff's voice came over the intercom as they leveled off at cruising altitude. "Gentlemen, this is your pilot speaking. We are now at cruising altitude; you can now unfasten your seatbelts."

Moments after they landed in Abu Dhabi, a convoy of sleek black vehicles pulled up to the curb, and Jeff escorted the Sheikh to one of the cars. Jeff took the seat beside him as the Sheikh settled into the back seat of the lead car.

As the convoy moved along the dusty road, Jeff's tension grew. He couldn't shake off the feeling that something was amiss. The landscape around them seemed almost too quiet, too still. He cautiously glanced at the Sheikh, who was engrossed in a conversation with his advisors.

Everything remained fine for now, but he knew something would happen; he could feel it in his gut.

Upon reaching Qasr Al Watan, the grand conference hall was abuzz with anticipation as Sheikh Rashid, resplendent in traditional attire, entered the room. The leaders from various nations had gathered for a crucial diplomatic meeting. As he took his seat at the head of the ornate table, the Sheikh's security team, led by Jeff, stood vigilantly at the corners of the room, their eyes scanning for any signs of trouble.

As the Sheikh addressed the gathering, danger lurked unseen.

Unbeknownst to the Sheikh and his security detail, a well-coordinated group of assailants had infiltrated the conference hall. Cloaked in the guise of attendees, they moved silently, biding their time until the perfect moment to strike.

As the meeting progressed, Jeff's senses remained razor-sharp. He had seen the subtle shifts in body language among the supposed attendees, the way their hands twitched, the nervous glances exchanged. His instincts sent him warning signals, a silent alarm that something was amiss.

"Team Alpha, stay alert. Something doesn't feel right," Jeff's keen eyes scanned the crowd for any potential threats. He adjusted his suit jacket and discreetly touched the earpiece in his ear.

"Copy that, Jeff. We're on high alert." A security team member replied through the earpiece.

As the Sheikh continued to address the gathering, Jeff discreetly moved his hand toward the concealed holster beneath his jacket. His fingers rested on the grip of his weapon, prepared for any eventuality.

"And I will end my speech . . . " Just as the Sheikh was about to reveal a groundbreaking proposal, chaos erupted. Gunshots echoed through the hall. The room erupted into panic as delegates and security personnel scrambled for cover. The assailants, armed with automatic weapons, began firing indiscriminately.

Jeff's training kicked in. With a swift motion, he drew his own weapon, his eyes scanning for the Sheikh amid the chaos. He spotted the Sheikh attempting to duck behind the conference table. He made his way quickly toward Sheikh Al-Rashid as he saw an assailant running toward him.

"Get down, Sheikh!" Jeff shouted, instinctively pushing the Sheikh's head down and reaching for his weapon. Bullets whizzed past, shattering the windows of the hall.

"Stay low!" Jeff ordered, returning fire with precise shots that took down two attackers. He kept the Sheikh shielded behind himself.

"Jeff, we need to get out of here!" the Sheikh yelled, his voice strained with fear.

Jeff quickly assessed the situation. Their best chance lay in reaching the nearby table for cover. "We're moving, Sheikh. Stay close and follow my lead!"

With Jeff in the lead and the Sheikh close behind, they sprinted toward the tables, bullets kicking up the windows and chairs around them. Jeff fired back, keeping the attackers at bay.

They reached the end of the room and hid behind a large marble display. Just then, more shots were heard echoing around, and Jeff knew they were soon to be ambushed.

"We need help," the Sheikh panted, his face pale but determined.

"Already on it," Jeff replied, speaking into his earpiece. He relayed their coordinates and the dire situation to their backup team.

The gunfire intensified, and it was clear the attackers were closing in. Jeff's mind raced as he weighed their options. He glanced at the Sheikh, his eyes filled with both resolve and gratitude.

"We'll make it through this, Sheikh. Trust me," Jeff said as he reloaded his weapon, utterly sure that his team was already in place to give him all the backup he needed.

The World Championship

◆———————◆———————◆

As Jeff opened fire, the assailants fired back. But unbeknownst to him, an attacker crawled behind him while his partners diverted Jeff's attention by firing. It was a setup so that one of them could crawl as quietly as a ghost from behind and execute the Sheikh.

The attacker, blade in hand, lunged toward Sheikh Rashid, a wicked grin etched across his face.

Jeff interposed in an instant, intercepting the dagger's path with his forearm. "What? Did you think I am that dumb?" He smirked as he punched the attacker in the face.

Pain seared through him, but his resolve was unbreakable. Gritting his teeth, he grabbed the attacker's wrist and twisted it, forcing the blade to clatter onto the marble floor. The assassins were surprised; their eyes widened as they saw their scheme unraveling before them.

"You won't succeed," Jeff growled, his grip firm as he held the assailant's wrist.

The room was a maelstrom of confusion, cries of shock echoing through the air.

The other security personnel swiftly apprehended the would-be assassin, subduing them amidst the chaos.

As the situation was controlled, Sheikh Rashid approached Jeff; his gratitude was evident in his eyes. "You saved my life," he patted Jeff's shoulder.

Jeff's muscles ached, and his arm throbbed from the impact, but he managed a humble nod. "It's my duty, Sir."

The Sheikh extended his hand, and Jeff, his battered forearm still smarting, shook it firmly.

Jeff's earpiece crackled as they shook hands, "The Security Team is ready to escort the Sheikh. Jeff, you may bring him out safely."

"Sheikh, we need to go. They might attack again." With that, Jeff took Sheikh Al-Rashid to his private helicopter, waiting on the roof of the building guarded by the security team.

"Jeff, we have somewhere important to go," the Sheikh said.

"What is it, Sir?" Jeff asked, curious about this new assignment.

"I want you to come to Leipzig for the World Championship. One of my fighters is participating, and I wish to be there to support him," the Sheikh explained.

"Of course, sir. I'll make all the arrangements for our journey to Leipzig," Jeff replied, mentally preparing for the trip.

However, just hours before they were about to take off for Germany, news came that the Sheikh's champion had refused to participate, leaving the Sheikh without a fighter.

The Sheikh looked disappointed, but he could not back down from a challenge. "Jeff, it seems my fighter cannot compete. What a pity," he sighed.

Jeff sensed an opportunity, a chance to make a difference. "Sheikh, if you permit me, I could step in and fight on your behalf. I have some experience in the fighting world," Jeff offered.

The Sheikh's eyes widened, surprised by Jeff's proposal. "Jeff, are you sure? This is not your usual domain," he said, concerned for Jeff's well-being.

"I'm confident in my abilities, sir. I have trained extensively my entire life," Jeff explained, eager to seize this rare chance.

After a moment of contemplation, the Sheikh smiled warmly. "Very well. You have my blessing. Make me proud." he said, placing a hand on Jeff's shoulder. "I am going to hire the best trainer for you. You know how to fight really well, and I am sure this trainer will teach you martial arts in two weeks."

As the trainer entered the room, before the introduction, both Jeff and his trainer bowed.

"Hello, Jeff, I am Kaito. I will be your trainer for the next two to three weeks."

"Training is really not necessary. I've already informed the Sheikh that I have been a master at martial arts."

"This is not a game, Jeff. It's a World Championship. I am here to bring out the best in you. I have seen many men as overconfident as you think that they can win at this, but they come back bruised and bleeding. So no, I don't believe that you are a master at this."

"Alright then, let's have a match right now. Then you will believe me?" Jeff scoffed.

"Alright, Jeff, challenge accepted," Kaito shrugged. Assuming that Jeff was being overconfident.

As they started the match, Jeff caught Kaito off guard and plunged him on the mat with one strike. "Now, Master Kaito, who is being overconfident here, me or you?"

"Alright, you can fight, but the match is not over yet," Kaito stood up.

"Are you saying you want to continue?" Jeff raised his eyebrows.

"Of course, I am." Kaito shrugged.

"Alrighty." Saying this, they took their positions and resumed what they had started.

Strike after strike, Jeff proved to Kaito that he was a master in martial arts.

As they finished, Kaito finally spoke, "You're a great fighter, Jeff. But still, we have to train until the match. Until then, you can keep beating me." Kaito chuckled and bowed, and Jeff bowed in response.

Jeff had already overcome incredible odds in the world of MMA. With five victories under his belt, he had proven himself as a force to be reckoned with in the championship.

Now, as he stood in the locker room before his sixth and final fight, the arena buzzed with anticipation, fans filling the seats, eager to witness a clash of titans.

The opponent he was about to face was no pushover. He was a skilled fighter with a reputation for brutal knockouts. He was hungry for victory and was determined to keep Jeff from claiming the championship. But so was Jeff.

Stepping onto the mat, Jeff noticed a beautiful blonde woman in the crowd, watching the match with keen interest. Her eyes were filled with determination and passion, and Jeff couldn't help but be drawn to her.

Jeff stood in the center of the ring, his heart racing fast as he faced his opponent. The lights above illuminated the arena, and the crowd's deafening cheers filled the air.

Across from Jeff stood a fierce fighter known for his incredible speed and fierce precision. Jeff could sense the tension in the air as they waited for the referee's signal to begin.

The bell rang, and they both bowed to each other. Jeff and his opponent circled each other, both aware of the stakes at hand, looking for openings. Jeff knew he had to be strategic to find the weakness in his defense.

The arena was alive with energy, the crowd's deafening cheers echoing in Jeff's ears.

His opponent struck first, a lightning-fast jab that Jeff narrowly evaded. Jeff countered with a powerful kick to his midsection, but he sidestepped, barely avoiding the blow. The crowd gasped at the display of skill from both of them.

The dance of combat continued, each exchange escalating in intensity. Punches and kicks were thrown with lightning speed, and the crowd's roars grew louder with each hit that landed.

They traded blows back and forth, neither of them giving an inch. The sweat poured from Jeff's brow as he focused on every moment, every opportunity to strike.

A powerful right hook came Jeff's way, and he managed to duck just in time, feeling the whoosh of air as it passed. Jeff retaliated with a swift roundhouse kick but blocked it with a well-timed forearm guard. The crowd erupted into cheers, appreciating the skill displayed by both fighters.

As the rounds progressed, fatigue began to set in. Each punch felt heavier, and every movement demanded more effort. But Jeff knew he had to dig deep to find the strength to keep going.

With the championship within reach in the final round, they both unleashed their most powerful attacks. Their fists clashed in a brutal exchange. Jeff felt the pain resonating in his entire body, but he kept pushing forward, refusing to back down. Then, Kaito's words echoed in his mind: "You have to be the tiger if your opponent is playing snake. You have to hold him by his neck, Jeff!"

Then, in a moment of opportunity, Jeff saw an opening and launched a devastating combination of strikes, catching his opponent off guard. A powerful uppercut followed by a hook sent him reeling backward.

Jeff swiftly evaded the second swing, embracing the tiger mindset. Unlike the other animal styles in the Shaolin Kempo Karate system, such as the snake, leopard, crane, and dragon, which often utilized defensive moves prior to striking, the tiger was distinct. Its approach involved relentless offense, mirroring the apex predator's dominance in nature. Jeff transitioned his stance as if gripping invisible tennis balls and lunged at his opponent. Jeff's fingers dug into his bicep while Jeff struck his forearm with the palm of his hand, like a tiger's paw. This maneuver followed an ancient Kung Fu strategy: target the attacking limb. The bat dropped to the ground.

Seizing the moment, Jeff went on the offensive. Employing Kempo Hands, Jeff executed rapid-fire strikes: a double palm heel to his ears, followed by a downward rake along his cheek, and then a strike to his chest. Stepping underneath his arms, Jeff thrust a strike into his abdomen, disrupting his center. Jeff lifted his leg into the air in an arcing motion and moved it inward to the center of the body, kicking with the inside edge of the foot. It was the Inward Crescent Kick. This continuous onslaught left him reeling, unable to counterattack effectively.

With his body jerking unpredictably, Jeff further disrupted his equilibrium with successive strikes. Blood spattered from his nose and mouth, and he collapsed in a gurgling heap. Unyielding, Jeff pressed forward, delivering a double palm heel strike at his opponent.

As he fell to the ground, his resistance crumbled, and he lay defeated, battered, and bleeding.

Jeff had previously clocked himself at six strikes per second, and if anything, the pace seemed even swifter at that moment. Initiating with a step reverse back kick and maneuvering underneath his flailing arms, Jeff strategically slipped in to deliver a roundhouse kick into his abdomen.

Flowing seamlessly, Jeff transitioned into a back fist strike at him. The sequence culminated in an arcing motion, targeting the bridge of his nose with another palm heel strike. The execution was fluid and efficient, devoid of any preparatory movements or superfluous actions; every motion flowed naturally into the subsequent one.

His body spasmed back and forth, syncing with the corresponding strikes of each attack. The fundamental tactic of Kempo Karate involved hitting an assailant in opposing ways, preventing them from regaining their balance to mount a counter-offensive. This approach also compelled the attacker's body to transition abruptly into the subsequent strike. The strikes seamlessly flowed into one another, generating a cascading effect. An external observer would perceive it as a unified whirlwind of motion, a rapid blur impossible for the eye to track.

Amidst this, blood sprayed from his nose and mouth. His eyes shut, emitting a gurgling noise as his arms flailed helplessly while he was propelled backward.

But Jeff's mindset was the tiger, an animal that kept going when it saw blood.

So, he took another step forward and chambered both his hands, palm forward, elbows bent: the left one at shoulder level; the right, at his hip and shouted a "Kiai"—the warrior yell, and launched a double palm heel strike, imagining both his palms penetrating through his body. He contacted his bladder and the underside of his cheekbone. They were both prime acupuncture points, but just as the meridians could be used for healing, the pathways could also be blocked.

His head whipped around, and he collapsed, lying on his back, bleeding from the various facial lacerations he had gotten during the fight. His lungs hurt, and Jeff coughed in fits.

This is how a deer might look after being taken down by an actual tiger. Completely shocked and overwhelmed by the ferocity of the attack, waiting for the neck bite that would end it all, Jeff thought. He saw his opponent was coughing but could finally breathe again without laboring.

Jeff pressed his advantage with the crowd on their feet, delivering a crushing knee strike that knocked his opponent to the mat.

But Jeff's opponent tried to rise to his feet. However, he was clearly shaken, and Jeff could see the toll the fight had taken on him.

When the bell rang, Jeff had won. The crowd erupted into thunderous applause. Their cheers filled the arena, adorning Jeff.

After the match, the blonde girl approach Jeff with a smile. "That was an impressive performance," she said, her voice as captivating as her eyes.

"Thank you. I'm glad you enjoyed it," Jeff replied.

"I couldn't help but notice your skills out there. I'm actually preparing for my 3rd-degree black belt test in Taekwondo, and I could use a good teacher," she said with a hint of shyness.

"I'd be honored to help you prepare," Jeff said, genuinely flattered by her request. The idea of teaching someone as dedicated and passionate as her was intriguing.

"Oh, thank you so much! You don't have any idea you've lifted a huge burden off me." She jumped excitedly. "Oh, and by the way, my name is Monica." She said with a grin.

"Hello, Monica. I am Jeff," Jeff extended his hand.

"Oh, I know who you are. The whole crowd was cheering your name." Monica chuckled as she shook his hand. "It seems you have to go now. Your team is waiting. We will meet at our practice," she smiled.

Basking in the glory of his triumph, Jeff made his way out of the ring, his body bruised and battered from the intense fight. He was taken for a thorough checkup, where the doctors attended to his injuries.

After a week, Jeff and Monica began training together. They met at the dojo.

"So, Monica, what got you into Taekwondo?"

"Well, I've always been fascinated by the discipline and control the martial arts require. Plus, the physical and mental benefits are incredible."

"I completely agree," Jeff nodded.

"By the way, your moves were so fluid and precise during the tournament. It's obvious you've dedicated a lot of time to your training,"

"Thank you. It's been a journey, that's for sure. And speaking of journeys, your upcoming 3rd-degree black belt test sounds like a significant one."

"Oh, it's nerve-wracking, to be honest. But having someone experienced like you as a teacher could make all the difference."

"Well, thank you," Jeff blushed.

"I'm excited to learn from you. And hey, maybe after all this training, I'll be able to give you a run for your money in a friendly sparring match!"

"I'd be up for the challenge, Monica. But for now, let's start with the basics and build from there. We'll work on refining your techniques and perfecting your form," Jeff chuckled.

"Alright, Jeff, let's get started. First, we'll work on your stance. Stand with your feet shoulder-width apart, knees slightly bent," the trainer explained.

"Like this?" Monica asked.

"Perfect. Now, imagine an invisible line running through the center of your body. This is your centerline. Your movements will revolve around it."

"Got it. Centerline."

"Good. Now, let's focus on your punches. Start with a basic jab. Extend your front hand, keep your elbow slightly bent, and snap it back quickly."

"Like this, right?"

"Exactly, Monica. The key is speed and precision. Now, add a cross. Pivot your back foot as you extend your backhand across your body. Generate power from your hips."

"It feels a bit awkward."

"It takes time to build muscle memory. Practice will make it feel natural. Now, let's move on to kicks. Begin with a front kick. Lift your knee, extend your leg, and snap it back."

"This kick seems easier."

"It's all about finding balance. Now, try a roundhouse kick. Pivot on your standing foot and whip your leg around. Keep your toes flexed."

"Whoa, that's a bit challenging."

"No worries, Monica. Rome wasn't built in a day. With practice, your flexibility and technique will improve. Now, let's combine some moves. Jab, cross, front kick."

Monica kept doing what Jeff instructed.

"Excellent! You're getting the hang of it. Remember, martial arts are about discipline and control."

"I'll keep that in mind."

"Good. Now, let's work on defense. Practice blocking and evading my attacks."

"Sure thing," Monica shrugged.

"When you block, use your forearms to protect your head and body. And when you evade, use footwork to create angles that make it harder for your opponent to hit you."

"This feels like a dance, in a way," Monica chuckled.

"Martial arts are a dance of combat. Now, let's finish with a sparring session. Apply what you've learned, but go easy. We're just practicing."

"Alright, I'm ready."

They engaged in a controlled sparring session, practicing the techniques they discussed earlier.

"Great job, Monica! I didn't know you could fight so well. But you must keep practicing, and you'll continue to improve."

Over the next few weeks, Jeff and Monica met regularly for training sessions. Their bond grew stronger as they practiced together. The more time they spent together, Jeff felt drawn toward Monica.

"You're really nailing those kicks, Monica. Your dedication is paying off," Jeff remarked, a smile on his face.

"Thanks, Jeff," Monica smiled.

"I can't believe how far I've come since we started this. Thank you for being such a great teacher, Jeff," Monica grinned.

"You've put in the hard work, Monica. I'm just guiding you. And honestly, spending time with you has been a highlight of my days."

"Are you saying you enjoy my company more than practicing your kicks?" Monica asked playfully.

"Well, let's just say our training sessions have become something I look forward to." Jeff laughed while gazing at her beautiful brown eyes.

3rd Degree Belt

J eff and Monica's training sessions became a daily routine, and the more time they spent together, the more Jeff's feelings for Monica blossomed. The dojo where they practiced Taekwondo had become more than just a place for training for Jeff. It was now a place where they met each other daily, not just to train, but Jeff could meet her, feel her presence, and spend as much time as he could with her.

Monica surprised Jeff each day. Many things about her made Jeff fall in love with her even harder. She even knew how to fly airplanes, which had come as a pleasant surprise. They occasionally took off on adventures on the private airplane that

Sheikh had given Jeff as a reward for winning the championship for him.

Monica was a superwoman, in his opinion, as he had never met any woman with such skills as Monica. She soon became his co-pilot, and he taught her to fly the aircraft even better. Her Taekwondo skills also flourished under Jeff's guidance, and he watched with pride as her kicks became more precise, her blocks more solid, and her movements more fluid.

One evening, after an intense training session, Jeff suggested they take a walk to unwind. "You look really tired, Monica. Maybe we should give it a rest for a while."

"Oh, thank God! Let's go, please, or I will die on this mat." She stopped her practice and tried to catch her breath.

"I have to show you something." Monica led him through the streets with the enthusiasm of a local, eager to share her favorite places in the city.

As they strolled through the cobblestone streets, passing by charming cafes and historic buildings, Jeff couldn't help stealing glances at Monica. Her vibrant smile illuminated the twilight, and he was captivated by how her eyes sparkled with excitement as she spoke about the city's history.

"You know," Monica said, her voice softening, "I used to explore these streets alone, imagining I was on an adventure. Look at this beauty, Jeff, the Thomaskirche," her eyes sparkled.

"What? This building under construction?" Jeff raised his brows.

"Silly, this is not just any building under construction. This is the remains of Johann Sebastian Bach!" She continued, "Thomaskirche is a Romanesque and neo-Gothic church dating back to the 12th century. After it was destroyed in World War II, the church underwent massive restoration. The remains of Johann Sebastian Bach have been buried in the Thomaskirche."

"Whose remains?" Jeff leaned in.

"Jonah Sebastian Bach, Jeff. You don't know him? He was a musician of the late Baroque period. He produced over 1,000 pieces of music, Jeff, 1000! He enriched established German styles through his skill in counterpoint, harmonic, and motivic organization, and adapting rhythms, forms, and textures from abroad, particularly Italy and France."

"Monica, you seem very impressed by this dead person. Do you want me to dig his grave and take his skeleton out for ya?" Jeff chuckled.

"Well, I'll be grateful if you can. I'm gonna hug him," she smiled back.

"Come, I have another place to show you. It's just a five-minute walk. We can drink coffee there as well." Monica jumped from the bench they were sitting on, grabbed Jeff's arm, and dragged him along.

They walked for about three minutes, and there it was Monica's favorite place, Zum Arabischen Coffee Baum. At the entrance, an Asian man was sitting in front of a tree offering a coffee to a young Westerner, like the old East initiating the West to coffee.

"This coffee shop is the oldest coffee house in Europe, dating back to its opening in 1720. It is named after a sculpture above the entrance portal that dates back to 1720 and remains well-preserved today. It is also a free museum with 500 artifacts documenting the history of the Saxons' love for coffee." Stepping inside, Monica explained a brief history to Jeff as her eyes moved desperately to watch this beautiful place, even though she had come here a thousand times.

"This museum is dedicated to Saxony's special role in the history of coffee culture in Germany. Drinking coffee was a way of life in Saxony. Frederick II is said to have shaped him with this quote:"

"Ohne Kaffee mangelte es den sächsischen Soldaten an Kampfmoral und sie verweigerten den Einsatz mit dem Argument ‚Ohne Gaffee gönn mer nich gämpfn."

"Ahhh, sad! If only I knew German," Jeff mocked playfully.

Monica laughed. "It means 'Without coffee, the Saxon soldiers lacked morale and refused to go with the argument, I don't want to fight without coffee.'"

"How come we've been winning Taekwondo matches all along without coffee, Monica," Jeff grinned.

Monica chuckled at his jokes.

"Come, let's have a coffee, and then I'll give you a tour."

"Alright." Jeff nodded and took the lead, walked toward the table first, and pulled away the chair for Monica so she could sit. "My lady."

Monica took her place at the seat. "Oh, thanks, Jeff. After weeks of rigorous training with you, I forgot that you could be a gentleman." Monica grinned as she mocked him playfully.

As the waiter came, Monica ordered for them both, "Zwei coffe Baum spezial, bitte." She smiled at him, and the waiter nodded as he made his way to the counter.

"What did you say to him?" Jeff asked, leaning towards her.

"I said, 'Two coffee Baum special, please.' It's their special coffee, Jeff. You're gonna love it." She was excited to share her favorite drink with him.

"I'm sure I will." Jeff gazed at her sparkling eyes.

After drinking their coffee, Monica gave Jeff the tour through fifteen museum rooms, which included more than 500 artifacts and audio and film exhibits illustrating the history of Leipzig's coffee house culture and Saxon's coffee culture. Jeff glanced at Monica during the tour, and he realized that Monica was in love with this museum and all the places she took him in Leipzig; she admired every inch of this city.

As they continued the tour, Monica stopped at a point. "Napoleon drank coffee in this cup in 1813." She pointed at a rusty cup resting in the cabinet. There were other artifacts, including roasting utensils, coffee brewing pots, coffee house rules, "Blümchenkaffee" (weak coffee), and a sample roaster.

But for Jeff, the most precious thing in that museum was Monica. She was a sight to behold, and he admired her fierceness, dedication, kindness, and spirit. He had never met a woman like her in his entire life. Since they had started training together, his feelings for her had grown stronger. Being with her had become the highlight of his days.

As Jeff helped Monica get her black belt, his journey was marked by unwavering dedication and a thirst for constant improvement. What began as a personal passion in his childhood had evolved into something far greater. Jeff's ranks grew stronger with each fight, training session, and obstacle he faced.

As Jeff continued to train and teach and represented Sheikh Al-Rashid in multiple combats, he found himself drawn to becoming a Grandmaster in Taekwondo. It wasn't a decision made lightly but a natural progression of his lifelong commitment to the art. Thus, with determination, he set out to achieve this lofty goal and kept participating in the Taekwondo combats.

The Sheikh was also really happy with Jeff as he won every combat he represented the Sheikh in. He had become the ultimate champion who was unbeatable. The Sheikh couldn't be prouder and grateful as he had one of the best fighters as a bodyguard and in the World Championship.

Sheikh Al-Rashid even increased his pay and awarded him with expensive cars. Jeff was living a perfect life.

His belt color had already advanced with each victory, and he had reached the 6th Dan. Jeff embarked on his journey in the world of competitive martial arts with the same determination he had shown in his role as Monica's trainer.

Monica, who had become more than just a student to him, was always there in the stands, cheering him on with the same enthusiasm he had shown her.

Jeff and Monica were surrounded by the faint scent of worn-out mats and the echoes of their months of training, standing in a quiet corner of the dojo. It was the day before Monica's Taekwondo competition.

Monica's excitement was palpable, but so was her nervousness. Her hands trembled slightly, and her gaze flitted between her uniform and the tournament schedule.

Jeff noticed her apprehension and placed a reassuring hand on her shoulder. "Hey, Monica, listen to me. I've seen you fight; you're the best student I ever had." He paused and remembered something. "God, you even smashed me to the ground once, remember? You're ready for this." He chuckled, trying to cheer her up.

She raised her brows and laughed, "You were distracted at that moment."

"But still, you were able to put me to the ground," Jeff shrugged.

Monica smiled but still seemed uncertain. "I know, Jeff. It's just that . . . what if I mess up? What if I freeze on the mat?"

Jeff stepped in front of her, making sure his eyes met hers. "Listen to me, Monica. Doubts are normal, especially before a big event. But you've trained tirelessly for this. You've faced challenges, pushed your limits, and grown stronger daily. Remember all those times you overcame obstacles during our training? This is no different. You have the skills, the strength, and the determination. And guess what? I'll be right there, cheering you on."

Monica nodded, "Thank you, Jeff."

Jeff smiled warmly. "You've done the hard work, Monica. Now, let's talk about focus. When you step onto that mat, I want you to block out everything else tomorrow. Don't worry about the audience, the other competitors, or even the outcome. Focus on yourself, your techniques, and the countless hours you've spent perfecting your moves. Each kick, each block, they're second nature to you now. Trust your training."

Monica took a deep breath, her confidence slowly returning. "You're right. I need to trust myself."

"Absolutely," Jeff affirmed. "And remember, nerves are just a sign that you care about what you're doing. Embrace them, but don't let them control you. Turn that nervous energy into determination."

Monica's eyes sparkled. "I won't let my nerves get the best of me. I'll give it my all."

"That's the spirit," Jeff said, a proud smile on his face. "And no matter the outcome, remember that this competition is just a checkpoint in your journey. Win or lose, you're still growing, still learning. And I'll be here, cheering for you every step of the way."

The arena buzzed with energy as Monica stood at the edge of the mat, dressed in her crisp white Dobok. Jeff stood nearby, his eyes filled with pride and encouragement. "Remember what we talked about," Jeff whispered, his voice steady. "Focus on your techniques, stay sharp, and trust yourself."

Monica nodded, a mixture of excitement and nerves churning within her. "I've got this, Jeff."

The referee's whistle blew, and the match began. Monica's opponent, a skilled practitioner with a determined look in her eyes, mirrored her across the mat. The crowd's cheers faded into the background as Monica tried to focus.

The first round displayed calculated moves, both fighters testing each other's defenses and finding openings. Monica executed her kicks and blocked precisely, her body moving with fluidity from months of relentless practice. Her opponent matched her blow for blow, creating a dance of power and strategy.

Jeff's voice rang out from the sideline, his words a steady stream of encouragement. "Keep your guard up, Monica! That's it, capitalize on her openings!"

As the second round commenced, Monica's determination intensified. She felt the burn in her muscles. Every kick felt like a step toward victory, and every block was a shield against defeat.

The final round arrived, and Monica's focus was unbreakable. She remembered all the early mornings, the hours of sweat and sore muscles, and the countless times Jeff had pushed her to be her best. It was all culminating in this moment.

With a swift spin, Monica launched a roundhouse kick that caught her opponent off guard. The strike landed cleanly, earning her valuable points. Her opponent retaliated with a combination of punches and kicks, but Monica's training had honed her reflexes. She blocked, dodged, and countered, never losing her poise.

As the seconds ticked away, Monica found herself in a perfect position for a high kick, a move she had practiced tirelessly. She seized the opportunity, her leg shooting up with power and precision. The impact was flawless, and the crowd erupted in applause.

The match concluded, and Monica and her opponent stood side by side, the intensity of the battle replaced by mutual respect. The judges conferred, and the final decision was announced: Monica was the winner.

Tears of joy welled up in Monica's eyes as she bowed to her opponent and then to the audience. She turned to Jeff, a radiant smile on her face. He approached her with open arms, enveloping her in a tight embrace.

"That was great, Monica! I think you're ready for your 3ʳᵈ degree black belt test."

Monica's heart swelled with pride and accomplishment. "Thank you, Jeff. I couldn't have done it without you." She hugged him even tighter, and for the first time, she felt something for Jeff, maybe even more than he felt for her.

"You were the one in the ring, Monica," Jeff replied. "You showed determination, skill, and heart. This victory is all yours."

This win was more than just an achievement; it was a testament to the hours of practice, the setbacks overcome, and the belief that she and Jeff had in her abilities.

The test started at 8 p.m. It was a Friday in the studio. About two dozen family members and friends sat on fold-out chairs inside the front door and watched as their loved ones, dressed in white uniforms, were joined on the wooden floor by ten other students and nine black belts who were dressed in all black. Jeff was among them, sitting on the fold-out chairs.

As the studio members called it, the support network, or community, was emphasized in Peakean as it is a significant part of the test.

The test involved ten stages; the first stage was the warm-up with a bunch of jumping jacks and stretching. Then Monica performed each belt's kicking combination up and down the studio.

For the third stage, she had to do a lot of push-ups. With twenty push-ups at the white belt, Monica kept adding ten push-ups for each belt she already had, so she did 100 push-ups during the test.

She went through all the belt forms in the fourth stage. She was doing just fine with everything up until the fourth stage. Jeff wasn't worried for a moment as he had complete faith in her abilities. Monica had spent months perfecting her Katas. She knew them by heart and could perform them with her eyes closed. She had broken countless boards with her powerful strikes, honing her breaking techniques to perfection. Her sparring skills had been tested and proven against formidable opponents, even earning her a few tournament victories along the way.

But the black belt test was the ultimate challenge. It would require her to perform all the Katas she had learned, demonstrate her breaking techniques, and spar with other black belts to prove her mettle. The stakes were high, and the panel of higher-ranking black belts would be watching her every move.

As for the push-ups, Monica had to do sit-ups with each belt, starting with twenty until she did 110, till the brown belt, making her do 150 sit-ups during the test, and the same went for the squats.

Now was the time for sparring; she had to do three rounds of sparring. The first two were against one black belt, and each round lasted one and a half to two minutes. She went up against two black belts during the third round for about two minutes.

Yes, she took a lot of beating. Why sparring at the end of the test? Because any martial arts-trained person can fight fresh, the black belt shows that a person can fight even when exhausted, and this was exactly what Monica had to prove.

Monica faced off against other black belts, each one a formidable opponent. She moved with agility and strategy, countering their attacks and landing her strikes.

After a while, the sparring session ended. Monica was exhausted, but she had given it her all. She looked to Jeff, who nodded with pride.

At the grand finale, Monica did hand-breaking with five thick boards. She lined up in front of a row of wooden boards, each thicker and tougher than the last. With a fierce yell, she struck each board and shattered them into pieces.

The panel of higher-ranking black belts nodded in approval, acknowledging her skill and dedication.

Monica's heart pounded as she waited for their decision. Finally, one of them stepped forward with a black belt wrapped around his waist.

"Monica," he said, "you have shown remarkable skill, determination, and spirit throughout this test. You have proven yourself worthy of the black belt, and we are proud to award you the 3rd-degree black belt."

Monica's heart soared as she was filled with joy and relief. She had achieved a significant milestone in her martial arts journey. She returned, running to Jeff, and jumped into his arms to hug him.

"You did it, Monica. You earned that 3rd-degree black belt," Jeff said, his voice full of emotion as he hugged her tightly.

Monica was now a 3rd-degree black belt in Taekwondo and got what she wanted. "Come with me. I have something to show you. I planned a celebration." Jeff held her hand.

"A celebration? You were so sure I was going to win, Jeff. Aren't you the sweetest?" She smiled warmly.

"Well, I'm afraid I might just be." Jeff shrugged, a mischievous smile on his face.

"Let's go now, or we're gonna be late." Jeff dragged her out of the arena.

He took her to the Auerbachs Keller, a restaurant in Leipzig that had roots dating back to the 1400's when a wine (or at least the historical equivalent of a wine bar) sat on the same spot in Leipzig. The bar and restaurant evolved over the centuries, even notably becoming one of Johann Sebastian Bach's favorites, who was Monica's favorite. Jeff had hoped the upscale restaurant would impress her, not that he thought it would be her first time there. It seemed a perfect spot to bring her and tell her about his feelings. Jeff opened the car door for her as they approached, and stepping outside, she was in awe. "You chose this restaurant, Jeff? This is just perfect!" She covered her lips with her hands in awe. "This was . . . " As she continued, Jeff interrupted, "This was Johann's favorite restaurant!" He finished her sentence.

"Awe, you knew. You thought this much about my special day, Jeff. I'm so glad I have you as a trainer and friend in my life."

"And I'm glad I had you both as a student and a friend." Jeff gazed at her with love.

The restaurant was intimate and elegant as they entered: a dimly lit space filled with dining tables, a piano bar, and jazz music. Nothing was out of place; every flower was pruned to perfection, every tablecloth pressed within an inch of its life. It was just the perfect atmosphere for his confession of love for her. They sat in a small booth, and from how he eagerly drank the water as soon as it arrived, Monica could tell he was nervous. *Is tonight the night he will ask the one question I have waited eagerly for?* She wondered.

"Jeff, are you okay?" Monica asked, her eyes furrowed as she tried to hide her smile.

"What?"

"I'm asking, are you fine?"

"Yeah, yeah, I'm absolutely fine," Jeff shrugged.

"If you say so."

"Well, there is something, actually." He stuttered. "Monica, I ... I ... "

"I what, Jeff?" She leaned in closer, her eyes fixed on him.

"Monica, I've been meaning to say something to you for a while now. But I was waiting for the perfect moment, and I think it's the perfect time."

"Yes, Jeff, I'm listening," her heartbeat quickened.

"Monica, we have spent each day together for over a year, and I . . . " His phone buzzed as he was about to express his feelings and infinite love for her, and its screen flickered with the private number calling. Jeff frowned as he knew who it was. "Sorry, I gotta take this call," Jeff said and hurriedly stepped outside the restaurant.

The Call

Jeff fidgeted nervously with his phone while Monica was still inside the restaurant, her eyes fixed on him. She had been waiting for Jeff to speak all day, but that call ruined their evening.

"Hello?" Jeff answered the call in a low voice.

"Jeff, it's Smith. We've got another assignment for you," the voice on the other end of the phone spoke.

"Smith, can't someone else do it? I'm working as a bodyguard for a Sheikh here, and it's a really good job. I can't leave it. I'm finally making a life for myself."

Jeff tried to persuade Smith by mentioning the job he got there, but truth be told, he wanted to stay back and be with Monica.

"This is urgent, Jeff. We need you to bring in a high-profile criminal by air. It's a level-seven assignment." Agent Smith sounded serious. "You signed a contract with us, and this is really something only you can do. We will pay you good money, better than that Sheikh is paying you."

"Alright, Smith. Give me the details," Jeff sighed.

"That's my man." Agent Smith continued. "The target is Juan García Ábrego."

Jeff was shocked, "Juan Garcia? The one on the FBI's most wanted fugitive list?"

"Yes, he's the one. He's currently holed up in a remote location by the Mexican government. We've managed to trace him there."

"But how did you trace him?"

"Mexican police arrested Garcia Abrego on a ranch outside of Monterey."

"I'll get the necessary gear ready and depart immediately. What's the extraction point?" Jeff asked.

"You'll need a rendezvous with your team at the private airstrip outside the city. We're sending you the target's location and coordinates. Be prepared to take off within a few hours."

"That soon ... ? I need a day at the least to tie up some loose ends."

"We don't have the luxury of wasting a day, so no can do! Whatever it is, leave it be and be ready for the next set of instructions."

Jeff nodded as he knew the drill all too well. "Fine! I'll be there. Send me the details."

"Remember, Jeff, this one's a priority. We're counting on you." Agent Smith stated firmly. "We need him brought in safely and without a trace."

The call ended, and Jeff returned to the table, his appetite gone.

"I'm so sorry," Jeff apologized as he took his seat at the table.

"Is everything alright?" Monica asked.

"I'll explain later. Let's finish our dinner first." Jeff managed to bring a smile to his face.

"You were saying something to me before you left to get the call." Monica raised her brows.

"Oh, it was nothing important." He couldn't tell her now that it was ruined.

As they finished their dinner, Jeff nervously traced the edge of his glass. The time had come to explain his real work that he had kept concealed for so long from her.

"Monica. I'll be leaving soon. Duty calls!" Jeff said hesitantly.

"Why?"

"Monica, there's something I need to tell you. Something I've never talked about before." He kept moving his fingers on the glass edge.

"What is it, Jeff?" Monica leaned in. "Is it about that call? You've been acting weird since then."

"It's just . . . my work, it's not something I can easily share."

Monica gazed at him; her eyes filled with curiosity.

"Whatever it is, Jeff, I'm here for you. You can trust me."

Jeff took a deep breath, his eyes searching for the right words.

"I work for Special Security, Monica. It's a classified division that deals with sensitive matters, national security, and investigations that are kept out of the public eye." Jeff confessed. However, it wasn't the confession he thought he would make before coming to the restaurant.

Monica's eyes widened; her surprise evident. She never imagined Jeff was involved in such secretive work.

"I had no idea, Jeff. What do you do for them?" She placed her hand gently on Jeff's, encouraging him to continue.

"I received a call just now. They've assigned me a mission that requires me to leave immediately. I don't know how long I'll be gone." Jeff explained, guilt-ridden.

"Oh." Monica's eyes were now filled with sadness and disappointment. She had expected a different conversation tonight that might have brought them closer together.

"Jeff, I thought . . . I thought tonight was going to be different. I was hoping you . . . you would." Monica's eyes teared up, frustration and sadness creeping into her expression. "Never mind. Let's just forget it."

"Monica, I wanted to tell you something important, but this call . . . it couldn't wait, and now I don't think it is the right time to say anything more. I promise I'll explain everything when I get back."

Monica nodded, blinking back her tears, her heart heavy as she hoped they would be united today. Their love remained unspoken, but it was a force that neither of them could deny.

"Can't they find someone else, Jeff?" Monica asked with hopeful eyes.

"I did ask them about that, but it's my responsibility. I can't just walk away from this."

"I promise we will talk. But right now, I have to go."

Monica took a deep breath, thought, and leaned closer to him. "Then I'm going with you," she said with a smile.

"What? No, Monica, it's too risky," Jeff was startled.

"I can't keep waiting, wondering if you'll return. If you're involved in something so dangerous, then I want to be a part of it with you."

"No, Monica, I can't let you. It might not be safe."

"I'm not asking you, Jeff, I'm telling you."

"Are you sure about this?"

"I've never been surer of anything in my life, Jeff. I want to be by your side, no matter what."

"Why do you want to come with me, Monica? Why risk your life?"

"Because you're my trainer and friend, and I don't wanna lose a good friend." She hesitated as she tried to hide her feelings.

"Monica, this person I must transfer from Mexico to the U.S. is dangerous. I can't take you with me just because I'm your friend."

"C'mon, Jeff. You've seen how good I am in martial arts. I can break the bones of bad guys," Monica smirked.

Jeff's smile widened; he had seen her fight and knew that she could beak bones of men twice her size. "Alright." He chuckled.

"Alright, as in, I can come with you?" Monica asked, her eyebrows raised.

"Yes." Jeff nodded. "But before you get too excited, you must know the rules. You'll keep a low profile and stay hidden, okay? Promise me you'll stay close and be careful. I can't bear the thought of anything happening to you."

"Alright, alright, I will." She rolled her eyes and then looked at him again. "Thank you, Jeff." She held his hands tightly.

"So, tell me about this assignment of yours. What mission are you going on?" She took a sip from her glass of wine, knowing she would go with him, and finally relaxed.

"Sshhhh! I can't talk about the confidential missions in public, Monica; what is wrong with you?"

"Oops, sorry," she smiled embarrassingly.

"Let's go. I'll tell you in the car." Jeff stood up and grabbed his coat.

As they drove together, Jeff finally broke the silence, his eyes on the road ahead as he began to speak about his mission. "We have to extract Juan Garcia, a Mexican convicted drug lord. He is the world's most wanted drug kingpin and is also tied to dozens of killings and other crimes. I must bring him to the U.S. for his trial." Jeff continued. "He is the leader of Gulf Cartel, a criminal group in the state of Tamaulipas."

"What kind of other crimes?" Monica asked, looking directly at Jeff.

"Well, he exports marijuana from Mexico into the U.S.. He's also involved in car theft activities. He is basically known for innovating Mexican trafficking operations and turning them from smugglers to suppliers. Our forces have estimated that Garcia Abrego smuggles over 300 metric tons annually across Mexico and the United States border."

"Tell me more," she encouraged Jeff, eager to hear the details of the mission and, perhaps, the chance to draw closer to Jeff.

"Tomas Mortel, the police officer in an elite Mexican police force, turned into a national trafficker and exchanged hash with Garcia Abrego. You know what happened to him?" Jeff paused long, "That officer was later found dead."

"No way!!" Monica was shocked.

"He was shot twice in the back in the doorway of a restaurant in Mexico."

The more he spoke, the more their connection seemed to deepen. It seemed as if the trust they had built over a year and the undeniable chemistry that had always simmered beneath the surface were all coming together at that moment.

As they continued down the open road, Jeff's voice became softer, more intimate, as he said, "Monica, I couldn't have asked for a better partner. You've always had my back, and I . . . "

Before he could finish his sentence, Monica reached out and gently touched his arm. Her voice was equally tender as she replied, "Jeff, I feel the same way. You've always been there for me, too."

As Jeff and Monica's eyes locked in that intimate moment, the world around them seemed to disappear. Without another word, Jeff gently pulled the car to the side of the road and turned to face Monica. Their hearts raced as they leaned closer, both of them on the brink of finally voicing what had been lingering between them for far too long.

"Monica, I . . . " Jeff began, his voice trembling, his heart pounding heavily in his chest. He leaned in closer, determined to finally express what had been on his mind for so long.

But just as he was about to say those three life-altering words, his phone buzzed, breaking the spell that had enveloped them. It was a call from Sheikh Al Rashid's manager.

As he spoke with the manager, Monica watched him silently, disappointment and frustration etched on her face. The moment they had shared, the confession that had been so close, had been stolen away.

"Shit! I have to go with the Sheikh. How could I forget!" Finally, Jeff ended the call.

Monica sighed softly, her eyes reflecting frustration.

Jeff put his phone away. The moment was lost but not forgotten. He turned back to Monica, a wistful smile on his lips. "I'm sorry, Monica. Duty calls, as always."

She nodded and managed a weak smile. "It's okay, Jeff. You do your duty, and I'll start preparing for whatever lies ahead."

Jeff pulled the car back on the road. Once again, his love confession was interrupted by a phone call. He cursed inwardly yet smiled, looking at a determined Monica by his side. She was going with him, he couldn't believe this, but at the same time, he was happy at this turn of events.

Confession

66Monica, are you sure you're ready for this?" Jeff turned to Monica, who was, at the moment, his co-pilot.

"Jeff, I am sitting on your co-pilot seat. Why do you think I am here?" She scoffed. "Obviously, I am ready to go."

"I am just asking if you're sure that you want to come with me before taking off. You know you can get off this plane anytime."

"Jeff, I didn't board this plane to get off it." Monica winked. "Don't worry, I know how to protect myself, and besides, you'll be there with me."

"Alright then, here we come, Mexico." He shook his head and got ready to fly the plane. "By the way, you're just gonna distract me there."

"Oh, I would never." She chuckled. "I'll be as silent as the grave."

The private jet was now in the air.

"Jeff?" The radio crackled; Smith was on the other end. "Share your position with me and the estimated time you will reach Mexico."

"Alright, I'm going to send you the details. But Smith, Juan is a high-profile criminal, so I want you to make sure I have backup. I can't risk it this time like we did the last time with Manuel Noriega. I have something extremely precious that I will protect with my life."

Monica's eyes widened. She turned to look at Jeff, but he kept his face expressionless. She knew he was talking about her. She felt that she had finally met someone who would never give up on her and would never let her go.

"Jeff, do you have someone with you right now? You know that these missions are confidential. You're not allowed to tell anyone."

"Smith, just consider this person as a partner, and I need her by my side to ensure everything goes smoothly. Don't worry; she can be trusted."

Monica kept wondering if Jeff would confess; it was the right time, but Jeff would never confess a thing as big as this on such a mission, and she knew that she had to step up this time.

Jeff gripped the controls. "We're approaching the Mexican border," Jeff announced, his voice calm but tinged with anticipation. "Monica, make sure you're ready for anything."

Monica nodded; her eyes fixed on the radar screen. "I've got our radar systems online, Jeff. We should be able to avoid any unwanted surprises."

As they neared the border, Jeff reached for the radio and spoke in a hushed tone. "Smith, this is Jeff. We're crossing into Mexican airspace. Keep an eye on us and be ready to provide backup if things go south."

Smith's voice crackled through the radio. "Roger that, Jeff. We've got your back. Stay safe."

As Jeff descended, the wheels of their jet touched down on the sun-soaked tarmac of the Mexican airstrip. Jeff maneuvered the plane to a stop, and the engines powered down. They had made it safely to Mexico, and there was still one more day before the extrication of Juan Garcia from the Mexican authorities. Jeff and Monica prepared to exit the plane as the engine's noise subsided. Jeff turned to Monica, "Well, we've got some time before we have to get to work. What do you say we explore Mexico a bit?"

Monica's heart leaped at the prospect of spending the day in Mexico with Jeff. After all, she could always spend some alone time with him. She couldn't suppress the smile that spread across her face. "I think that's a fantastic idea, Jeff."

"Great!" He smiled back, and they disembarked from the plane and stepped onto the Mexican soil.

"There's your bedroom." Jeff pointed at one of the rooms that were just a wall apart as they entered the safe house, "And this one's mine." He pointed to the room next to hers.

"And why do you get to decide?" Monica raised her eyebrows.

"Because this one's is closer to the main gate, and if someone breaks in, my room would be the first one they'll enter." He shrugged. "I don't want you to get hurt, but if it makes you uncomfortable you can take this room."

Monica was embarrassed, "I was just asking, that's all. I'm cool with this room. Okay, see ya later." She hurriedly entered the room and slammed the door behind her.

Jeff chuckled, shook his head, and entered his room.

For an hour, Monica rested and came out of her room, dressed in a man's button-down shirt, denim shorts, and black track shoes. Her hair was tied up in a cute ponytail, and a strand was hanging out on her face.

"Ready already?" Jeff looked at her as he flipped the steak in the pan. "I made lunch. Let's eat first, and then we'll go out."

"Oooh, I didn't know you cook." She was impressed. "But Jeff, we were supposed to rest for an hour, didn't you rest?"

"Nope. I thought that today, I'll bless you with my delicious meat." Jeff paused, "It didn't sound that bad in my head." He laughed.

"Here you go. It's done." Jeff placed the steak in front of her and then took a seat across from her with another plate of steak.

"I'd love to try your meat," Monica said playfully as she poked the fork inside the steak.

After having lunch, Jeff went inside his room to change his clothes, and Monica cleared the plates from the dining table. They were going out in the streets of Mexico for the entire day since they had to extradite Juan the next day.

Jeff came out of his room wearing a black T-shirt and denim shorts. "Let's go." He grabbed his backpack from the chair and made his way to the exit door.

Venturing on the streets, they witnessed enticing scents of street food and the distant ocean. They strolled through the colorful markets, sampled street tacos, and admired the city's intricate architecture.

Monica was a history lover. The historical places, ruins, museums, and monuments excited her more than anything. He knew the right place to take her to, "Museo Virreinal de Zinacantepec," in a former Franciscan convent. He remembered Monica mentioning this place; she was passionate about it when she told him that she always wanted to come here.

Just when they were about to reach it, Jeff covered her eyes with his hands. "I've got a surprise for you, Mon." He led her in front of the museum and removed his hands from her eyes.

"Oh my God, Jeff." Monica was in awe, "This is amazing. You're on such an important mission, yet you remembered that I always wanted to come here. Oh, I am so glad to have you in my life." She paused as something clicked in her mind, "This is why we came a day early? Isn't it?"

"Well ... " he shrugged.

"You're the best." She kissed his cheek.

Jeff blushed, "Come, let's have a look inside."

As they entered the museum, inside the main entrance was a vestibule leading to the abbey's main courtyard. A magnificent 16th-century mural was set above the low main door into the abbey. The Tree of Life illustrated the Franciscan Order's history and its martyrs.

"I want to see the famous baptismal font." Her eyes scanned the area as she entered, "Where's it?!" she whispered.

"What's baptismal font?" Jeff kept gazing at the Tree of Life.

"Ahhh, the baptismal font is the jewel of this museum, Jeff. It is the largest monolithic sculpture of its kind, which shows a religious narrative of Tequitqui art, which accounts for the Franciscan and indigenous syncretism."

Jeff kept gazing at her; he loved her enthusiasm, the excitement with which she was talking about the sculpture. "Lost you at sculpture, Mon," he chuckled.

"Ugh." Monica paced forward, frustrated with him. The abbey had two floors and housed the exhibits of the museum. As she moved, she saw several large rectangular panels along the corridors, largely consisting of monochrome depictions of saints like Peter and Paul and martyrs like St. Lawrence and St. Sebastian. There was a variety of mural ornaments in the form of polychrome, grotesque bands, and patterned wall decoration where she finally found the sculpture she was so eager to see.

Jeff kept following her, loving how she was deep in her zone, which was history and art. Her eyes sparkled, and she was the happiest around such places. He kept falling for her harder each day. She was just amazing. She knew martial arts, was a 3rd-degree black belt holder, and knew so much about history. *She could also be a historian with that passion and enthusiasm,* he thought.

Suddenly, Monica stopped walking. "Jeff, come look at this. This was the sculpture I was talking about." She was thrilled. "Oh, I wish I could hold it."

"Oh no, no, no. You'll get us into trouble. Let's just get out of here, or you're gonna steal this thing." He dragged her out of there.

As they moved further, there was a collection of sacred art and an extensive documentary collection, which displayed the time's religious, political, and social development.

Finally, they ended their tour, "We've explored your dream place, now let's go to mine." He held her hand, and they walked outside the museum.

"Where are we going, Jeff?"

"We are going to the mountain, Nevado de Toluca."

"What? Aren't we going to be late?"

"Don't worry, we still have 24 hours." Jeff winked at her.

They were at the Nevado de Toluca, overlooking a breathtaking vista of the Mexican landscape and gazing at the stars. Monica turned to him. It was finally the moment to take her shot. "Jeff," she began hesitantly, "there's something I've been wanting to tell you."

Jeff turned to face her, his eyes locking onto hers with intensity. "What is it, Monica?"

Taking a deep breath, Monica mustered the courage to speak her truth. "I . . . I care about you deeply, Jeff—more than as a friend. I've been hiding my feelings for a long time, and I know you are doing the same, but I can't keep it a secret any longer. I know you wanted to say something to me and were interrupted. Something tells me that you wanted to tell me about your feelings." She paused. "Jeff, I . . . I can't imagine living without you now. I never imagined I would be so much in love with someone, but I can't stop falling for you."

Monica had imagined it thousands of times in her mind before coming up with the right choice of words. When she said she loved him, it meant she loved him to the core. When she decided to confess her feelings for him, she risked losing even the friendship she had with Jeff.

Because, believe it or not, nothing remains the same after that one confession.

Jeff wasn't ready for this; he was shocked that Monica felt so much for him. He knew there was a spark between them, and she cared about him, but he couldn't imagine that she would be so much in love with him.

Jeff's heart skipped a beat, his feelings for Monica echoing in her words. He cleared his throat, trying to find the right words. "Monica, being here with you is everything I could ever want. I try to find reasons to be with you, and the thought of leaving you behind in the Gulf and coming here to Mexico was poisoning me until you said that you wanted to come here." He chuckled softly. "I was afraid that you'd meet someone and I'd lose you." Jeff held her hand tightly, never letting go of them.

Monica blushed, her gaze dropping to the ground briefly before meeting his eyes again. "I'm glad you feel that way, Jeff."

Their eyes met, and in that moment, words became unnecessary. The moonlit night seemed to immerse them in a world of their own. Jeff's fingers gently brushed a strand of her hair behind Monica's ear, his touch tender.

Jeff leaned in, and they drew closer to each other, their unspoken feelings finally coming to fruition. In that moment, with the world as their witness, they shared a passionate kiss that sealed their love.

The next day, Jeff and Monica stood in the courtyard of a government building. "So, what happens when we reach the U.S.?" Monica asked.

"We hand over the prisoner to the State."

"Jeff, I'm asking about us." He raised her brows.

"Oh." Jeff realized. "Well, we're gonna return to Dubai to our prior jobs and continue practicing martial arts."

"Jeff, stop teasing me and give me the right answer." She hit him with her elbow.

"Alright, alright." He chuckled. "We'll talk about it when we get back home. They're bringing Garcia." Jeff pointed toward some government officials and guards who were bringing Juan Garcia to them.

"Yeah, we better, Jeff." Monica composed her professional face.

The moment of extradition had finally arrived. The legal proceedings had been initiated, and now it was a matter of ensuring Garcia was handed over to the American authorities.

Jeff, standing beside Monica, exchanged a knowing glance with her. The Mexican officials approached their paperwork in hand and began to read Garcia his rights in Spanish.

Jeff stepped forward, holding out the necessary documents for extradition. "Señor Garcia, these documents state that you are being extradited to the United States to face the charges against you."

Garcia's gaze finally shifted from the ground to Jeff's face. For a moment, their eyes locked, and he could sense a hint of desperation in his demeanor. But Garcia remained silent.

The Mexican authorities proceeded to handcuff Garcia, securing him for transport. Jeff and Monica kept a close watch as he was led away, their mission nearly complete.

As they escorted Garcia toward the waiting transport vehicle, Jeff scanned the area carefully to see if anyone was following them, but he did not sense any trouble. He was on high alert as he knew that Garcia remained a dangerous man, even in custody.

Just as they were about to board the aircraft, the sound of approaching vehicles rang in their ears. She turned to see a convoy of vehicles speeding toward them, their headlights piercing the darkness.

Jeff's expression hardened as he muttered, "This doesn't look good, Monica. Get ready for trouble."

Jeff unholstered his sidearm as he scanned the approaching convoy. Then, he noticed the men spilling out of the vehicles, armed and dangerous, clearly here to rescue their leader, Juan Garcia.

The goons, led by a burly man who appeared to be their enforcer, surrounded Jeff, Monica, and Garcia. Guns were pointed in their direction, and one of the goons quickly thrashed down Jeff, snatched his earpiece, and crushed it with his foot.

Juan Garcia grinned menacingly, even though he was under arrest. "You honestly believed it would be that simple, didn't you?"

Jeff's jaw clenched, but he kept cool as he was still held on the ground. "We did what we had to do, Garcia. Your time has come."

As they attacked, Monica and Jeff fought side by side, though clearly, they were outnumbered and couldn't hold out much longer. Although some of the men were down, Monica and Jeff both were exhausted now, and they knew it wasn't wise to keep fighting as eventually they'd be outnumbered.

"Monica, now is the time; you'll have to do it right now!" Jeff instructed as the situation got worse. He had already instructed Monica that between his and her life, she would have to choose to run for her life.

"Jeff, no." Tears welled up in her eyes. "I can't."

"Mon, do as I say, please!" Jeff managed to say as he fought.

He had already prepared her for this situation. It took her little time to understand that for Jeff, her life was more important than his own. She nodded with tearful eyes.

Just as Monica was about to turn, one of the assailants collared Monica beside him with his left hand and lifted her. He hoisted her in front of his body. He kicked her down on her knees and pointed his rifle at her. Jeff paused as he saw her in trouble. Yes, she was good in karate, but these men were no ordinary goons or street fighters. They were trained assassins.

"Come and get her!" he sneered as he grabbed Monica by her hair.

Monica managed to kick him in the leg, which made him lose his grip on Monica. Jeff took the opportunity and rushed toward him. He swung a powerful strike. His punch was strong, making the big man spit blood and roll over like a cat, gasping for breath as Jeff kept kicking him.

"Monica, take Garcia and go!" Jeff shouted. But how could she go now? She ran toward Garcia and took him to the plane. She waited for Jeff as she saw the rigorous fight between the two.

The assailant, scrambling to his feet, picked his hands out of the dust, butting Jeff in the chest. Jeff then charged again and caught the assailant with two long swings to the head. His skull roared with pain and dizziness. Jeff then prepared himself and started to swing in a blind fury, both his hands going with every ounce of power he could muster. "How dare you touch her?" He slid his arm around the assailant's thick neck, grabbed his wrist, jerked up his feet, and sat down with full force, trying to break his neck.

But the big, burly assailant knew all the tricks; he hurled his weight forward to the left, which broke the hold, and he rolled free. Finally, he came to his feet, but Jeff lashed out with a kick for his head. The assassin rolled away from it and hurled himself at Jeff's leg. Jeff fell, and as they scrambled up, Jeff hit him left and right, splitting his right cheek and splitting his lips.

"You're a big girl's blouse," Jeff said.

It was a term Jeff had picked up when he worked with a British man for two weeks on Sheikh's trip to England.

"And you're a turd." The assassin wiped the blood oozing out from his nose with his sleeve. He was bloody and battered now. His breath wheezed as he kept coming at Jeff. His face darkened. He seemed to swell up. He exploded at Jeff and launched himself forward with his right arm scything around in a giant roundhouse strike. Jeff sidestepped, and his body ducked under his arm, bounced up again, and spun around. He stopped short on stiff legs and whipped back toward him.

He came at Jeff again. Jeff crashed an elbow into his side as the assassin spun under his arm and came right back at Jeff, but he dodged away again and felt the breeze as his giant fist passed an inch above Jeff's head.

Jeff punched him on his left cheek and whipped a right uppercut to the body. The assassin gasped as Jeff circled him like a lion circles his prey. He smashed him in his stomach with a kick, then another and another. The assassin's face was battered and bleeding from a dozen cuts and abrasions. Jeff gave him his final bone-crushing punches, and with a thud, the assassin fell to the ground.

Another assassin came up behind him and struck him with a rod like a battering ram. Perhaps Monica cried out, but Jeff only saw her open mouth.

Jeff grabbed him by his shirt and yanked him so violently that he tore it off the right shoulder and kept striking him until he fell down. Jeff kicked him many times until the assassin passed out.

Just when violence seemed inevitable, a roar from above drew everyone's attention. The sound of a helicopter approaching rapidly echoed through the night. The goons hesitated, momentarily distracted.

With impeccable timing, Smith, their backup, descended from the chopper, armed and ready. He shouted commands at the assailants, urging them to drop their weapons. But they started to fire, and in response, Smith's team fired back.

In the chaos that ensued, Monica and Jeff ran to take cover, but Monica fell to the ground. Jeff pulled her up and took cover behind the aircraft. A brief but intense firefight erupted. The goons were overwhelmed; they were shot, and one by one, they surrendered or fled into the darkness; some even died.

As the dust settled, Smith approached them, his helicopter hovering nearby. "You know what to do … take care of Garcia."

Jeff nodded and gestured for Monica to board the plane. Monica nodded and, together with Smith, boarded the plane. Left with Garcia, he propelled him toward the plane, but just as he was ready to strap in, Jeff took out an unlicensed revolver and shot Garcia to death, pushing his crumpled body away from him. Jeff took his seat in the pilot seat, and Monica looked at him with astonishment. "Why did you kill him? He was supposed to be extradited?"

"Seems like you didn't tell her everything," Smith mocked.

"Monica, I'll tell you all about it later. For now, just know that we've completed the mission." Jeff announced as he prepared the plane for takeoff.

The Wedding, the Death

Monica's gaze was fixed on the clouds outside as they fled miles above the ground. Jeff could feel the tension in the air but was unsure how to break the ice. This mission had begun with excitement, but now there was a rift between them, a silence as vast as the sky beyond their window. Monica was furious, and Jeff knew it. He had hoped that he would easily mend whatever had gone wrong, but it seemed Monica had other plans, and with Smith being there, it made it more difficult for him.

Finally, the aircraft began a slow and steady turn, tilting slightly to the right. The wind howled as it made its final turn onto the waiting runway and ended with a mild rumbling as the tires kissed the tarmac.

It had been a long flight, and Monica had not ceased to ask the same question repeatedly, "Why did you kill Garcia?" anger poured through her.

Jeff, who had been evading the question since they had boarded the plane, finally turned to Monica, "Monica, I've told you before that we've completed the mission. I'll tell you the details later."

Monica's eyes bore into his, "Jeff, I saw it happen. I saw you … I saw you kill a man," she felt her throat closing. "How can I forget that."

"Monica, please, just listen to me. I need you to understand why I did what I did."

Monica stopped pacing and turned to face Jeff, her eyes locked onto his, searching for answers.

"You killed Garcia, Jeff! You shot him in cold blood! How could you do that?"

Jeff took a deep breath, trying to find the right words.

"Jeff, I need answers," she implored as she felt a flash of irritation.

"Monica, the mission was to eliminate Garcia. He wasn't just some random person. He was a dangerous criminal responsible for countless deaths and suffering. The agency sent me to take him out because no one else could get close enough."

"Jeff, you promised me answers. Tell me, why didn't we hand him over to the government?" Monica was now seething.

"I understand why that would make you angry." Jeff hesitated, then took a deep breath. "There are things you don't know, Monica. Garcia's trial would have been lengthy and costly. Wasting taxpayers' money, and that's one thing the man doesn't deserve—to waste more resources. People died because of his drug trafficking; some died of a drug overdose, and he killed people for money and left their families devastated. He had to die. The government had to deal with him like this. There wasn't any other choice."

Monica's anger started to wane as she began to grasp the gravity of the situation.

"Why didn't you tell me? Why didn't you trust me enough to let me in on it?"

Jeff sighed, realizing that he could no longer evade the issue. He leaned forward. "Monica, I need you to understand that sometimes I cannot share the details until the mission is over. For instance, that entire standoff, the apparent murder of Garcia, it was all orchestrated."

Monica's eyes widened in shock. "What? But I saw it happen! I saw you ... "

Jeff interrupted, "I know it looked real, but it was all pre-planned."

Monica's voice quavered with disbelief. "But why keep it from me? Why make me believe that it was all real? You could've just told me."

"I wanted to, Monica. I really did. But it was classified information. Even I didn't know all the details until I got to the mission site. And then ... I didn't know how to tell you without putting you in danger."

Jeff hesitated; his gaze fixed on hers. "Because, Monica, the people who wanted him back—they're relentless. They wouldn't stop if he were still alive.

He had to die. For good!" Jeff replied, flicking a cigarette on the ground.

"So, you mean to say that Garcia had to die all along?"

Jeff nodded solemnly. "Yes."

"And Garcia's people who came to save him were not his men?"

"Yes." He nodded again. "But he was a criminal, Mon, he had killed thousands. My superiors sent me to kill him, not to bring him to the United States. This is what governments do. Not every criminal is brought to trial."

"And what about the other men you killed?" she asked.

"They aren't dead, Mon. Like I said, it was all orchestrated," Jeff replied with a stern face. "Only the one who touched you is dead."

"And why is that?" Monica's expression softened.

"You know why." Jeff caressed her cheek. "It's because I love you." He strode over to her with a wide smile. She laced her hands with his, and he noticed just how small they were now that her palms were pressed into his.

"I love you so much." She almost whispered and smiled at him with a hundred words behind her eyes.

He leaned in closer to her; his lips met hers. In that moment, nothing else mattered, no worries or fear, no past or future. There was only the heat of the moment, the electricity between them, and the pure, unbridled passion of their kiss. The world around them was meaningless. Nothing meant more than them; nothing in the world could hold more beauty than this moment.

Months passed, Jeff had an apartment in Dubai, and Monica had moved in with him. They were living the fairytale of their lives. Jeff was still working for the Sheikh, and they both were practicing martial arts. Monica had become a master as well, teaching children while Jeff taught the people with higher-ranked belts.

He decided to take her to dinner one night. It was the day Jeff was going to propose to her. As they reached the restaurant, he led her to a small table in a quiet corner. Most tables were empty as it was a late hour for dinner. He pulled out her chair, and she sat. He sat across from her. The only light around them was from a few candles. A waiter approached them and, without saying a word, poured them wine and left the bottle—no menus, as Jeff had already ordered in advance. There would be no interruptions from the wait staff aside from bringing and clearing, of course.

Jeff watched Monica as she took a sip of the wine. She noticed, "What? What are you looking at?"

"Just the beautiful woman sitting in front of me," he smiled.

Monica blushed. They locked eyes across the table, and everything around them faded away. They were in a universe of their own. Lost in the depths of each other's eyes. They barely noticed the waiter had placed their meal between them.

After they finished their meals, the waiter removed their plates.

A romantic song started to play in the background; it was Monica's favorite. Jeff stood up from his seat, his hands clenched in his pockets; one pocket held a small velvet ring box. Now was the perfect time to propose; he knew that as he had always seen it in romance movies. But there were so many questions left unanswered for Jeff: how did someone go about doing that? Do they just pull out the ring and ask? And the biggest unanswered question for him was, Will she say yes? His gut churned with anxiety.

"Monica," Jeff said finally.

"What is it, Jeff?" Her mind was buzzing with a thousand thoughts. *What was Jeff going to say to her?* She felt that her mind would explode if Jeff wouldn't say anything for another second. A cold, tight knot formed in her gut. What was happening?

Jeff whipped the box out of his pocket so fast that Monica couldn't make out what it was. He kneeled on the ground with the box in his hand. Monica's mouth widened, and her mouth gaped as Jeff sputtered, "When I met you, I knew I met my soulmate, and when I think about you, I know that no one else will ever hold my heart the way you do. Your eyes rule my heart, Mon, and I want to spend the rest of my life with you. Will you marry me? I can't imagine growing old with anyone else, nor do I want to."

Monica had her hand cupped over her mouth to try and hide her shock, but Jeff could see from her eyes that she was smiling. Slowly, she bobbed her head up and down in a nod and kneeled and kissed Jeff, waiting for him to slide the ring onto her finger.

It was an autumn wedding in the late afternoon, and the wedding venue faced the breathtaking sunset in Italy, where Monica had always wanted her fairytale to begin. At the end of each seated aisle, jasmine-scented candles hung from the naked tree branches. Roses lined the aisle as far as the eyes could see. They invited a small group of close friends dressed in beach attire.

There she was, in her best dress, a gorgeous white laced gown. Jeff looked dashing in his tailored suit.

Jeff began shaking his head, staring at her, a broad smile on his face. The guests turned slowly as Monica passed them. The bridesmaids, in green dresses, formed two rows at either side of the altar.

Monica walked slowly, looking like a goddess. As she reached Jeff, he gave her his hand, and she stepped up on the stage. The pastor gestured them both to stand face to face each other and began, "In the name of the Father, and of the Son, and the Holy Spirit. Grace to you and peace from God our Father and the Lord Jesus Christ."

The guests responded, "And also with you."

"Dearly beloved, we have come together into the house of God in the presence of the church's minister and the community. Your intention to enter into marriage will be strengthened by the Lord with a sacred seal. Christ abundantly blesses the love that binds you. Through a special sacrament, he enriches and strengthens those he has already consecrated by holy baptism, that you may be enriched with his blessing so that you may have the strength to be faithful to each other forever and assume all the responsibilities of married life. And so, in the presence of the church, I ask you to state your intentions."

"Jeff and Monica, have you come here to enter into a marriage, freely and wholeheartedly?"

Jeff and Monica both replied in unison, "I have."

"Are you prepared, as you follow the path of marriage, to love and honor each other for as long as you both shall live?"

"I am," they both replied.

"Since you intend to enter the covenant of holy matrimony, join your right hands, and declare your consent before God and His Church."

Monica and Jeff joined their right hands. It was time to exchange their vows.

Jeff spoke first. "I choose you. I choose to stand by your side and sleep in your arms. I choose to bring you happiness and nourish your spirit, and to grow and learn alongside you as life and time alter us both. I promise to laugh with you in good times and struggle alongside you in bad times. I promise I'll always be there for you in your historical adventures. Monica, I love you unconditionally, and I vow to love you forever."

Monica spoke, "I love you with my whole heart, with a passion that can't be expressed in words, only in kisses, glances, and years of adventure by your side. Jeff, you are my every dream come true, and I can't wait for the reality we get to build together. I choose you and promise to choose you as my husband every day we wake up. I will love you in word and deed. Loving what I know of you and trusting what I don't yet know, I give you my hand. I vow always to protect you from harm and to stand with you against your troubles. I give you my love. I give you myself, the good, the bad, and the yet to come."

As they exchanged heartfelt vows under the clear blue sky, there wasn't a dry eye in the audience. Their promises to love, cherish, and support each other resonated deeply with everyone present. It was a ceremony filled with love, laughter, and happy tears.

They exchanged rings and looked at the pastor for the signal.

"In the sight of God and these witnesses, I now pronounce you husband and wife! You may now kiss!" The pastor nodded as he smiled.

Friends and family toasted the newlyweds, wishing them a lifetime of happiness.

After the dance and the feast, it was time for them to say their goodbyes and start their new lives. They sat in the car and hit the road.

Monica, sitting in the passenger seat beside Jeff, smiled at him. "Let's stop for a quick meal. I am hungry."

"Yeah?" He smiled widely.

"Yeah," she chuckled.

As they drove past a hot dog stall, Jeff stopped the car and started to reverse. Just as he tilted his head back to reverse the car, suddenly, he heard a loud bang. The voices around him were dull outside as the loud banging dominated his ear. It felt like a flash of lightning and a crack of thunder. He turned his head back, and the smoke drifted from the window of his car. He checked himself. There was nothing on him.

And then, the most heart-wrenching thought came to his mind; he widened his eyes and held his breath as he looked at Monica beside him. As he did, he saw a bullet had punched its way through her neck, causing a hole that quickly filled with blood. Her clothes started to soak with blood.

She had become a target in the dangerous world that Jeff had tried to protect her from. Unbeknownst to them, one of Jeff's enemies had tracked them down in Italy.

Panic surged through him as he cradled her in his arms. "Monica, stay with me!"

Monica's voice was weak as she whispered, "I love you, Jeff."

Tears filled Jeff's eyes as he watched Monica's life slip away before him. He knew that the enemies they had made, and the secrets they had uncovered had led to this moment. The rider, who was behind them since they had left, flashed in front of his eyes. He was there to kill him, but as he turned his head to reverse the car, the bullet hit her. She fulfilled her vow to protect him and stand with him against troubles.

Monica took her final breaths; each second stretched on, a lifetime of memories flashing before her eyes. Her last breath was a gasp, a futile gasp for life in a world filled with darkness. As she lay dying, the metallic taste of blood filled her mouth, and Jeff's cries sounded like a forlorn farewell as her breath surrendered to the relentless grip of death.

He looked into her eyes one final time. Words failed him, but his eyes conveyed a lifetime of love and regret, a silent conversation only they understood. Tears blurred his vision as he held her lifeless hand, a torrent of emotions washing over him as he remembered their laughter, dreams, and adventures, which were now shattered.

With Monica's last breath, a fire ignited within Jeff. He had lost the love of his life, and there was only one thing left to do—take revenge. He would track down those responsible for Monica's death and make them pay for what they had done.

As he held her lifeless body in his arms, a solemn vow passed his lips. "I promise, Monica, I'll avenge your death. No one will get away with this."

The streets faded into the background as Jeff's heart filled with a burning determination. He would stop at nothing, bring those responsible to justice, and ensure that Monica's death would not be in vain.

The Hardest Goodbye

Just three days after their wedding, Jeff was conducting Monica's funeral in the Monumental Cemetery of Messina in Italy. He decided on an historical place as her final resting place since she would've liked it.

He gazed at her lifeless face resting peacefully in the coffin. The casket was draped in a white linen, Monica resting atop. He realized that he was looking at her face for the last time.

Jeff remembered the day they were discussing the places they would visit after the wedding in Italy. She wanted to visit this place for their honeymoon;

he remembered Monica suggesting, "We will also visit the Monumental Cemetery of Messina."

"A cemetery? C'mon Monica, why would we go to a cemetery on our honeymoon?" Jeff chuckled.

"Jeff, I have wanted to go there since I was a little girl; it's one of my dream destinations."

"I'm sure there would be some history behind it as well?" He raised his brows, and she explained.

"Yeah, there is." She smiled. "Leone Savoja used the slope of a hill located between the suburban Palmara and the area of S. Cosimo, Sul Modello di Mosella. It is a place of rest and enjoyment for both the living and the dead."

"Enjoyment, huh?" Jeff laughed at her thought.

He clicked back into the present as the minister began to speak; he could barely hear the words as he wanted to keep looking at her.

Jeff could not help but think about all that Monica had done for him. She had always been there for him, even when no one else was. And now, she had given him the ultimate gift of life. But it wasn't worth living without her. He would never forget what she had done for him. She was gone, but her memory would live on forever.

It was time to lift her coffin and lead it to the quiet grave.

As Jeff stood at the edge of the grave, his feet sank into the soft earth beneath him.

He clutched a handful of dirt in his fist, watching as the coffin was lowered into the ground. As the first shovelful of dirt hit the wood, his flashback continued.

"Oh yes, Jeff, it's an enjoyment." She continued. "The Cemetery of Messina is a garden of memory sculptures in which sculptors, painters, plasterers, and architects of the time could show their mastery. Everything seems to be inspired by a deep meaning and high aesthetic value, from low wrought iron gates for the delimitation of tombs to the most impressive monuments. In the cemetery, you can find expressive portraits and talking allegories related to life, death, but also to the profession of the deceased."

As he was standing, a hand pressed his shoulder gently.

"I'm so sorry for your loss," it was Smith. "If there's anything I can do to help . . . " he trailed off, not knowing what else to say.

Jeff nodded, his eyes red-rimmed and glassy.

He had always been a private person, and this was the most public display of emotion he had ever shown. He didn't know how to deal with it or how to express what he was feeling.

"She was a great person," Smith said quietly. "She will be missed."

Jeff nodded again, not trusting himself to speak.

"Smith, I need your help. I need you to find the man on the motorbike. It's crucial."

"But Jeff . . . "

"Smith, just help me locate him."

Smith leaned back, studying Jeff's face. There was a moment of hesitation in his eyes.

"Fine, I'll see what I can do. But you should know he must be hiding, knowing you'll try to locate him."

"I expected as much. Smith, I appreciate this more than you can imagine. I'll be waiting for any information you can dig up."

He turned away from the grave, knowing she would be at peace there. But he could not rest until her killers were finally rotting in hell. His expression turned as his rage fumed inside him.

After Monica's death, Jeff spent days finding the hitman who shot Monica. He was the only clue Jeff had at the moment, but in his gut, Jeff knew it had something to do with Juan Garcia's death. Smith finally found the location of the hitman's hiding hole through his resources and informed Jeff about it.

Jeff knew the killer wouldn't come out of his hole for some time, so he had to go inside and get him.

Entering the apartment like a predator, Jeff grabbed the back of the hitman's head and flipped him off the couch onto the ground. The hitman's cheek smacked the coffee table. He moaned, and rivulets of blood fell to the ground. He was snarling as he stepped back and guided his foot up under Jeff's ribs. Then, he stepped back, balancing his weight on his left foot, and threw his right fist out in a curved punch to his temple.

Turning ninety degrees to the side, Jeff brought his right forearm up to counter the blow, formed a fist with his left, and threw it at his outstretched jaw. He stumbled back, blood rushing from his nose. The hitman was in trouble, big trouble, and he was unaware of it until now.

"Tell me." Jeff punched the hitman. "Who the hell sent you to kill me?" Jeff said between the punches he was landing on the man's face. He wasn't even giving the man a chance to speak; his rage had taken control over him. Finally, he stopped and asked again, holding him by his color, "Now tell me," his nostrils flared.

"Rafael Garcia," he managed to say between the gasps. "Juan Garcia's brother." Blood spattered out of his mouth.

"Where is he?" Jeff shouted but did not get a reply, so he hollered like an angry bear, "TELL ME!"

"He . . . he's hiding in Sicily. He knew you would come after him after your wife's death."

"Where in Sicily?"

"I don't know. I swear I don't know."

Jeff didn't say a word to him, just stared into his eyes with rage; Monica's dying face flashed in front of his eyes.

"Please," The hitman raised his face as he requested, "forgive me."

"You killed my wife, dammit!" Jeff kicked his gut as he shouted, loaded his gun, and pointed at him. He was looking straight into his eyes with a cold, detached look etched on his face.

Jeff hit him two, three, four times. To his credit, the hitman was still conscious after that, though crawling on his knees and elbows on the ground,

The noises eventually stopped when Jeff decided to be merciful and end his suffering by shooting him in the head.

Jeff dialed Smith's number. It was almost a few hours' drive from Messina to Sicily, which was enough time for Jeff to plan his revenge and Smith to find Rafael's location in Sicily.

Jeff managed to dodge Rafaelo's men outside the building and entered.

Jeff glanced around the hallway, making sure no one was watching, and then took a deep breath before slipping in the apartment window. The door swung open, and he stepped inside silently, closing it softly behind him.

The apartment was quiet, with only the sound of running water coming from the bathroom. The carpet muffled Jeff's footsteps as he made his way down the hallway. He could hear the faint echo of Rafael's voice as he hummed a tune in the shower and approached the bathroom door. He reached out and turned the handle slowly, pushing the door open with just a crack. Steam billowed out, and through the misted glass of the shower, he could see the shadowy figure of Rafael, his back turned.

Jeff clenched his jaw, his fingers gripping the handle of the door. This was the moment he had been waiting for, the moment of reckoning.

As he entered the bathroom, the sound of the water was deafening, masking the noise of his approach. Rafael continued to hum, unaware of the presence behind him.

The gun in Jeff's hand lifted effortlessly, and he realized just how ready he was to fire it. He wanted Rafael to know why he was dying, so he called to him, "Hey, Rafael!"

Rafael turned, shocked to his core, as fear ran down his spine. He opened his mouth to say something, but before he could say anything, Jeff emptied his entire magazine into Rafael's mouth.

As Rafael's lifeless body fell into the bathtub, Jeff took out another gun from his pocket and emptied it into his chest. He knew he was already dead; he just wanted to take out his rage. But nothing in the world could bring Monica back. Jeff fell on his knees on the ground and sobbed. "I've done it, Monica, I've avenged you!"

As Jeff made his way through the streets of Sicily, his phone buzzed in his pocket. It was Smith calling.

Jeff answered the call, "Smith?"

"It's done, isn't it?"

"Yes, it's done."

"What now, Jeff?"

"I'm going back to the U.S.. It's time to leave this all behind me, Smith. There's nothing left for me here."

"And Dubai? What about your job there?"

"I can't go back there, Smith. Every street, every corner would remind me of her."

"Alright, Jeff. We'll keep in touch with you."

Jeff ended the call by saying, "Yeah, we'll see about that."

Love and Duty

Y ears Later ...

As Jeff lay in the hospital bed, his mind drifted back in time to the moment he retired from the Elite One in 2010. It marked the end of an incredible 36-year career in service. Those years had been filled with challenges, triumphs, and unwavering dedication. He had seen and experienced things most people could only imagine.

But as he reminisced, a heavy shadow loomed over those memories. The pain of losing Monica, the love of his life, was a wound that had never truly healed. She was gone, and her absence was a constant ache in his heart. He vividly recalled the day she had died. The world seemed to crumble around him, and the pain was immeasurable.

Returning to the United States had been a difficult decision, but it was one he felt compelled to make. He needed a fresh start, a new beginning that would allow him to escape the memories and emotions that had haunted him for so long.

He began flying for a corporation, a path that allowed him to keep his mind occupied and distance himself from the overwhelming grief he felt.

Despite all his training and professional achievements, nothing could mend the broken pieces of his heart caused by the loss of Monica. The pain was a constant companion, an unwelcome reminder of what he once had and what had been taken away from him. He often found himself lost in thought, reliving the moments they had shared, the laughter, and the love that had been so abruptly torn from his life.

His eyes welled up with tears at the memory of her.

Jeff's mind carried him to a pivotal moment in his life, transporting him into the past. He vividly recalled the time he stood gazing out over the sprawling cityscape, a panorama stretching infinitely before him. The city's vibrant energy was juxtaposed with the weight of the past, and the gravity of his current situation bore down on him like a heavy mantle.

As Jeff had looked out over the city, he had been acutely aware of the dual responsibilities that rested upon his shoulders. On one hand, he had his duty to the government, a career of 36 years of service to the nation. It was a life filled with challenges, triumphs, and sacrifices, a testament to his unwavering dedication. He had honed his skills to become a formidable protector, and he knew that countless citizens relied on him and others like him for their safety and security. The weight of their trust was a burden he willingly carried despite the enormous pressure it entailed.

On the other hand, Jeff had experienced the profound love he had shared with Monica, a love that had been torn away from him by the cruel hands of fate. Her absence left a void in his heart that seemed impossible to fill. It was the depth of his love for her and the anguish of her loss that had etched wisdom into his soul.

The lessons he had learned had transformed him. It wasn't just about being physically strong or capable, though those attributes were certainly important. It was the strength of character, the unwavering sense of duty, and the ability to make difficult choices for the greater good that truly defined him.

Monica's love had taught him about the power of compassion and empathy, and his government service had instilled in him the values of duty and honor.

He had faced the complexities of the world and understood that difficult choices often had to be made. Sacrifices, both personal and professional, were a part of the path he had chosen.

Now, as Jeff had just woken up after his second operation, his mind was filled with these thoughts. He couldn't help but reflect on the incredible journey he had been through over the past year. It all began with a series of bewildering symptoms that made him fear the worst—Alzheimer's or dementia. He couldn't remember things as he used to, and it was a source of profound anxiety.

His sister came from Tennessee to the rescue. She rushed to be by his side and decided it was high time for Jeff to seek medical attention. Little did they both know that their decision would set in motion a sequence of events that would change Jeff's life forever.

Upon arriving at the hospital, Jeff underwent a battery of tests, including a brain scan. The results were nothing short of shocking. The doctors discovered a massive brain tumor, and when they described it as being the size of two tennis balls, it was almost beyond belief. This enormous mass had been pressing against Jeff's brain for an indeterminate number of years, silently wreaking havoc on his cognitive functions and general well-being.

The medical team quickly sprang into action, explaining to Jeff the urgency of the situation. He was taken into the operating room, where a grueling nine-hour surgery commenced. The skilled surgeons painstakingly worked to remove the enormous tumor from his brain. It was an intricate and delicate procedure, and Jeff's life hung in the balance.

The surgery was a success, but the road to recovery was just beginning. Jeff had to face the daunting challenge of relearning some of the most basic functions, such as walking and talking. The medications prescribed to him in the aftermath of the operation brought their own set of challenges, one of which was the loss of his flying privileges. The medication, while necessary for his recovery, had an impact on his health that extended beyond the brain surgery.

But that was not the end of Jeff's medical odyssey. A year later, he found himself experiencing chest pains that sent him back to the hospital. The doctors determined that he needed a procedure known as a TAVR, a transcatheter aortic valve replacement. However, the attempt to perform this procedure was not without complications. They tried four times, and each time, the valve placement slipped. It was a disheartening setback.

After these failed attempts, the medical team had to change their approach. They informed Jeff that he needed to heal and regain strength before they could proceed with open-heart surgery. It was another significant ordeal for Jeff to face, and it came just one year after the brain tumor surgery.

However, regardless of his deteriorating health, Jeff couldn't help but smile about the fact that he had lived a meaningful and fulfilling life. To this day, he wouldn't forget how he'd felt standing at the crossroads of life; the sun dipping below the horizon. Elite One walked toward an uncertain future, his heart filled with both sadness and determination, knowing that his journey was far from over. The legacy of his life would live on forever. He closed his eyes with contentment, knowing that even with all these health issues, he had persevered against life and come out stronger than ever.

www.ingramcontent.com/pod-product-compliance
Lightning Source LLC
Chambersburg PA
CBHW022109310726
48972CB00007B/1952